This is a work of fiction. Names, characters, businesses, places, events and incidents are either the products of the author's imagination or used in a fictitious manner. Any resemblance to actual persons, living or dead, or actual events is purely coincidental.

Copyright © 2014 by Jude Baas

All rights reserved. No part of this publication may be reproduced, distributed, or transmitted in any form or by any means, including photocopying, recording, or other electronic or mechanical methods, without the prior written permission of the publisher, except in the case of brief quotations embodied in critical reviews and certain other noncommercial uses permitted by copyright law. For permission requests, write to the publisher, addressed "Attention: Permissions Coordinator," at the email address below.

Hero Worship Press
info@heroworshippress.com

Library of Congress Cataloging-in-Publication Data has been applied for.

ISBN 978-1496167736

For my mother

PART 1
THE BOY

We are healed of a suffering only by experiencing it to the full.

~Marcel Proust
(1871-1922; pneumonia, pulmonary abscess)

ONE

Present day

Could taking a child's life be justified?

The dust spiraled off Nobel's footsteps as he neared the shed. The summer had been dry, and he slowed to catch his breath. He was panicking.

Through all his years in law enforcement, he'd foregone his own interest to live up to the Midwestern pronunciation of his name. For eight decades, he'd lived in service. The truth was unavoidable. People weren't ready for what the boy could do.

"Mason?"

Olea stared at him from the house, framed by the kitchen window. She only used his Christian name when she was nervous, and she had a right to be.

The shed latch had rusted shut. Nobel struck it with a hammer to free it, and the mania he was riding showed itself in a surge. The handle throat felt solid in his grip. His fingers had respited arthritis.

"The boy didn't mean anything by it. Can't you just quit

and come inside?"

Nobel lifted the sagging shed door to clear the ground and pulled at it. No one knew the boy was born. Beyond the three of them, the child didn't exist. His death wouldn't strain a thread in the social fabric.

Nobel knew his living certainly could.

The shed was windowless. The sun cut stripes through any shadow unwashed by the open door. He pulled the tarpaulin from the machine, like a magician pulling the cloth from a set table. The curdled dust suspended like satellite debris until gravity caught up.

The world was cruel at worst, at best dangerous in its indifference.

He topped the tank with diesel made from corn he'd grown in their fields, cleaned the brush arm, and replaced it.

Children were dispatched everyday. Inebriants and vehicles alone stole sons and daughters without shame, he said to himself, and noticed his eyelids collect like a gutter.

He was old and getting weak, and the boy was growing bigger and faster.

Nobel pulled the starter rope and the generator sputtered doddery to life. The exhaust had a salty taste, and he salved the cracks in his hands with a cloth of walnut oil. He'd scrubbed the solar panels with lye and pig fat soap that morning, but had forgotten his gloves and his skin had replied with eruptions of pus. The voltaics ran the refrigerator and charged the panel of truck batteries that took the night shift, but to use any other appliance required special occasion, and more juice.

The wood axe was butt-out underneath the front porch steps. Nobel wiped a cobweb from its elbow. Every molecule tugged at him to carry it in.

He could see Olea's silhouette at the screen door. Her posture disputed his gut's authority. They'd endured a lifetime of silences, but neither could quiet his viscera.

"I hear your shouting hush."

"The child loves you, and I care for him the same."

"Do I feel less?"

"That is what I'm asking."

"You could save an abandoned pup, Olea, and foster it to devoted maturity at your breast and not feel a fiber of the rope binding me to that boy."

The current between them said more was coming, and his saying it would make it meaningless.

"He is my soul unspoiled."

"Yet you have no belief in him."

"We don't know what's in the boy, and I will be damned before I abandon him."

He felt his face and lungs burn like the earth had tightened its orbit.

Olea took the smallest of his fingers and squeezed it. An udder to syphon off his embarrassment, Nobel thought.

"He wanted to see the highway, that's all."

"For now."

"He said he was sorry."

"He could run away at anytime."

"I don't want to talk about that."

Nobel measured his breath.

"Neither of us knows when we'll overstay our welcome, Olea, but it'll come sooner than the boy's lifetime."

The screen door was heavy on her shoulder, but she refused to give up his hand. He held the axe in the other.

"It's unfair to make me the sole voice against faith."

"Only if faith knows less about what's coming than you do."

"He'd suffer less if we left him bound to a tree, to be devoured by wild dogs. You're giving me a look that says, 'Yes, but-' and precedes something, so finish."

"You're not a man who can see the future. So how can you be sure?"

Nobel's chin fell as if her words were weight in his skull, and he shook it like he was saying *no* to scratch his breastbone.

"You're a woman in all parts but your tongue, which is a knife."

TWO

The boy could hear their talking.

The stovepipe ran a thin vein from his cellar room to the roof. Nobel'd carved out the basement from the hardpan below the house, sculpting the walls like he'd seen the Choctaw men do in his childhood, hauling down buckets of loam mud and fescue and pouring it into molds of chicken house plywood three hands wide on each side.

The labor is proof of something, he said each time he descended. It was a prison, but they knew better than to call it that. It was the boy's fortress. The one window was fit with bars made from cultivator parts. Petrified bones set tighter than his head, protruding from volcanic crag, the boy imagined.

The boy had his own pump works and a bowl made from a colliery bucket with a hole in the bottom and a cork stopper. A few pulls filled it like a cistern he used to drink and bathe when they decided it was unsafe to use the bathroom upstairs. He could hear Nobel shuffle through the house above. The dull thuds and scratch of boxes lugged and overturned meant he was looking for a bottle.

The boy sat on the floor, his pants already covered with soil from the week's work and play. Washing day was tomorrow so a bit more filth didn't matter, he'd decided. He kept his room clean but the clay was raw and would always mark. His bed was small but matched his size and had a frayed horsehair rug beside it, so he could walk barefoot without bringing dirt into the sheets.

He could see a stack of drawings he'd done on magazine pages hidden below the tavern table he used as a desk. Most were of the farmstead's animals drawn over dated faces of public figures and articles he'd been taught to read. A few were of landscapes composed on foreign backdrops. He spread them out and counted seven of Nobel and Olea, sketched onto photographs of medications and alcohols. He found just one of himself. It was charcoaled atop a block of text beside a picture of a dragonfly. With pollen and a beet rind rubbed on for color, he remembered. He'd sat in front of the silvered glass that leant beside Olea's closet, and stenciled his likeness with a carpenter's pencil Nobel'd given to him.

His doppelgänger looked content, and he arranged his legs and hands precisely, turned his shoulders and curled his mouth into the identical smile, and felt comforted by the companionship.

It was warm so his window was open and a breeze brought in the feather and perspiration smell of the chickens running outside, spooked by a buzzard. That had the circling shadow of a failed aircraft, the boy thought, and forced himself not to recall the incident. He'd read or been read all the books and bibles in the house, some more than once, and still didn't know what to believe. Was it possible an irregular thing possessed him? He couldn't feel it. But the defect could be unnoticeable, since he'd never lived without it.

Like a stink that disappeared because it was always there. Or was he a blind thing being told his color wasn't preferred?

They did know what was natural better than he did.

The boy could hear the generator. Its hum meant the voice was coming. He'd recognized the girl's sound immediately, he'd said the first time, but Nobel told him that was unlikely. He couldn't remember any other details, so hadn't argued.

Her accent was different than his. *Yokel,* Nobel called it, and the boy learned what that meant. It didn't suit her, he thought, and reclined on his back to address the ceiling, and waited for her birdsong to ease him.

Olea listened from the kitchen. She refused to join Nobel when he drank to endure a rising flood. Since they found the tape, she'd witnessed it just once. Enough to never forget.

Their tube television still worked because it came from an era that respected longevity, Nobel told himself. He sat on a camphor wood chest in the storeroom, and filled his stomach with corn liquor a mouthful at a time. One more viewing of the boy's mother might instruct him. The image was pixilated. The girl was no more than sixteen.

"This video is for you, Grandma and Grandpa," she said and her voice cracked, as a memory slipped through.

Her hair was oily and dyed yellow, and her cheeks were flushed and scabbed. So were her knees and hands. As if she'd hit the asphalt more than once. She smoked a found cigarette as she spoke and looked as normal doing so as a baby playing with an icepick.

The camera moved as she did, because someone was working it.

"Quit your twitching," the cameraman said like a drunk

scolding a dog, but with the clipped diction of education. His arm reached across the lens and he slapped the girl's leg.

He was older, Nobel had deduced. Folds of skin gathered at the cameraman's bones, and burns and liver spots pocked his hand like slugs crowding a dead leaf. Ink tarred each second knuckle making his fingers into ivory keys that had been jaundiced with nicotine. A cornice of tattoo coiled his wrist, corkscrewed to the elbow, and the remaining flesh was ice-white and frosted with rash. Nobel knew every boil on the limb and nothing else.

Are you the father? He mumbled like it was his line in the play.

The girl took the stained cigarette from her mouth. Smoke drifted between them and she lay back on a mattress puddled with sweat rings and tugged stuffing through an ulcer in the fabric. The hovel was so choked with detritus, livestock would've refused it.

"I remember you, Grandpa," the girl whispered and drifted within herself, compressing her lips, and then she held up a weathered picture.

The photo was of Nobel in a suit holding a five-year-old, whose little girl face was hidden somewhere behind the mask of the teen gripping it on screen.

The camera moved closer and the shadow of the man behind the lens covered her like a blanket, large and stooped with a Gorilla's paunch.

"I have other memories too," she added and as if on cue the cameraman tossed a coin purse at her. The clutch was tattered but held the remnants of a beaded poodle, and the girl removed a needle kit from inside like it was a Christmas stocking.

"My very favorite vein used to be the top of my foot. It was so precious and perfect and beautiful, until I missed with a shot of coke and now it's a twig."

The girl took a candle from the floor and cooked as she spoke. "I've decided to try my femoral with you. It's a dangerous vein, Grandpa."

She filled the syringe like a seasoned nurse and spoke like to a child.

"First I locate my heart's pulse, halfway up my thigh near my gash. Then I press my index finger just to the side of my heartbeat, and I slowly slide the needle into it."

The needle tip was large on screen and lingered deep in her skin without breaking its shell.

"Tell Grandma not to worry and that I love her."

Nobel watched, transfixed.

Before she thumbed the plunger, the girl looked at the cameraman and with a baby's inflection she asked, "Are you the devil?"

No reply came, from the cameraman or Nobel.

The lens shifted and her face grew to fill the TV screen.

Droplets slipped from the girl's eyes like crowded children pushed over a ledge. The corrosion washed from her face and she was as clean as a treasured doll again. Her breathing slowed and she disappeared, to a better place, in her mind alone. The tape ended and the screen became black.

"She was a pretty thing. I wish I'd met her sooner."

Olea could see Nobel bent forward from where she stood but couldn't see the recording. He looked like a lizard crimped on a clothesline and left to dry in the sun.

"Show yourself if you want to goad me." Nobel's voice was molten.

"You believe you failed to save her, so she coupled with a monster."

Nobel looked at her, but said nothing.

"Just like your mother, and you blame the boy."

"A mother bear slays the runt to save it from suffering, and to protect the litter."

"Is humankind your litter?"

As an answer he stood and walked to the cellar door. His empty bottle spun on the floor behind him like a revolver.

Nobel entered the basement room, a puppet to his madness, and Olea trailed like a gown's train. It smelled like wet dirt and mildew.

"Why, Papa?"

"I don't know."

Admitting so gave Nobel pause, and he laid his fingers on the boy's.

The boy's wrist didn't resist but had the strength to, and reminded Nobel he was an old man. The boy's hand was thin. There was soil under his small nails. His skin was young and pale pink. A child's derma seemed impossibly soft, flawless and alien beside an old man's starfish, leathered by the sun.

The axe blade severed the boy's part at the wrist at an untrue angle. Plasma swells gathered at the laceration and the vessels billowed, stemmed momentarily, their ends pinched like a bent straw by the bevel. The meat of the boy's arm bubbled and pooled on the desktop like a sponge squeezed, but no more. The mortal geyser declined to arrive, refusing to spurt the total of his blood at the rhythm of his pulse, like a faulty sprinkler head.

Nobel grabbed the boy's forearm, drug him across the floor and shook the stump like a pontiff's scepter as rage rode his slimed cheekbones in waves to his tongue.

"If ye were of the world, the world would love his own: but because ye are not of the world, the world hateth thee!"

His sputum fell to the floor in stringy dollops. His lungs were deflated pig bladder balloons and his voice lost its timbre.

Limp in Nobel's grasp the boy's eyes rolled back white in his skull, and he passed out. His bare belly rose and fell with his breath and the drip of jam from his stub slowed to a stop like a river frozen.

Olea used the room's echo to cluck the beat of a hymn like a didgeridoo, and Nobel turned axe butt over handle, seized its head for support and gathered the small, stray hand no longer of use to man or child.

Her muffled chanting ridiculed him as he walked to the barn and threw the piece into the pig's trough.

Nobel stepped away before the sounder made a meal of it but thought he heard the throaty pop of bone in their snuffling even from a distance.

Olea's *Leaning on the Everlasting Arms* drowned out all else as he reached the homestead's waterworks and stooped at the windmill's pump discharge to let the water chill his head and rinse his hands.

Her cantor act faded to a hum as he entered. She snapped peas undistracted at the kitchen sink, as if to prove there was no spell he could cast.

"What if you're not able?" She said and wiped her hands on her apron.

"Haven't I protected you with my every atom? Can a man love in a finer way?"

"You've answered a question with two of your own." Olea took a sealed jar of liquor from beneath the sink and set it on the countertop to mock him.

"I've not gone mad. I love the boy. To know what I do and to choose to do nothing, for my own contentment, would mean there's nothing greater than a man."

Nobel's emotion reached its levy as he waited for her to look at him.

"If that's the truth, Olea, why would I preserve anyone's stay in this world?"

"While you decide a fate for all of us, Mason, I'm simply asking you to consider something."

She delayed to be certain he'd hear every word.

"What if the boy can't be killed?"

THREE

Nine years ago

The amount of blood would make it difficult to forget.

Olea had picked up the kitchen table and set it atilt, wedged beneath a chair back so the planet's pull would assist. Her strength had surprised him. He'd built the table from planed fence posts. It was as heavy as a tractor tire. Adrenalin, he thought, and set the young woman on the slope. He was not the man he once was but the girl had malnourished herself to a weight he could bear. If this were the only good fortune they'd get, he would accept it.

The young woman gurgled sounds he couldn't understand, even with an ear at her lips. Liquid in her lungs, Nobel guessed. His grandfather had passed with pneumonia. It was a rattle that stuck with you. She choked on a word he couldn't make out. "Please" seemed likely. He caught himself suspecting she'd done so to lure him close again. Her inflated belly like the rest of her was smeared with road lard and coated with a gumbo of dust and particulate. Swollen abscesses spread like mating leeches red and glazed on her arms and across her chest. Her lips were split crackers. Her teeth were caked with a brown film. Nobel knew her. He recognized her right away, in spite of the wear put on her. She was his wasteful son's child, their one grandchild. Her skin was taut and bruised, her nose and ears pierced and connected by a thin chain, but she had the eyes she was born with. Eyes Olea shared and her father as well.

Nobel had put arms around her only once before. She'd perched in his lap as a five-year-old. That was the age they'd told him and that her name was Ella, Ella Nobel. She'd gripped his forefinger tightly with her small hand, he recalled, and leaned her tiny head into his chest, as if to leave an impression. Her hair hadn't been cut since birth, and she smelled of animal sweat and honeysuckle from an afternoon of chasing wild mousers through the vine plants that sweatered the house porch. The social worker that brought her took a photo. Even then her doughy face and blueberry eyes threatened the beauty she'd destroy or be destroyed by soon, Nobel thought.

Their son had killed himself and her mother the night before by steering into a Bur oak that proved immovable. A skilled drunk, he'd delivered them both through the windshield and to the bone yard, Nobel recalled saying, when they still entertained company. He and Olea were too old to foster the child and envisioned the county finding her superior care in a younger, more modern pair of replacements. That was their goodbye, and the irony of her parting gift brought back fourteen bleak years later didn't escape him upon reflection.

She groaned in parturition now. Her lungs emptied and struggled to refill like an unseen presence stood on her ribs.

"This birth will be bad," Nobel said involuntarily.

The skull crown of her new son was pressing toward a kitchen floor shared with the feral cats they kept for rat catching and his desert beast dog, Bill.

Nobel'd seen creatures born before. He'd delivered twin calves, horses breached and still born and even a backward mule once. Human births made him weak-kneed. He'd always left his sows to fend alone in their final moments of delivery because of the resemblance. Maybe it was a childhood thing. He didn't have the patience or occasion now to think on it more than that.

Olea spread her granddaughter's legs like opening a damned life's double doors and gaped as the gore flowed milk thin with clotted kernels of sloughing rot. The girl huffed and Nobel took her hand into his like a tatting of twigs. As if awaiting this moment, she fastened her eyes onto him. He brushed a tangled of hair from her brow. Sweat and tear beads cut trails through the dirt on her cheeks and slid from the frontier of her skin to the table's rough surface. Olea busily cooled towels she'd boiled and gathered what birthing tools she had. With a dank cloth and his free hand Nobel cleaned the girl's face of crud and secretion. She gripped his free hand in hers, looping her fingers around his first, tightening them. Nobel kept hold, took the weight of her small head in his other palm and her skull collapsed in surrender, like she'd held out for this touch. Her eyes clouded, dispelled and open and her body writhed up like a snake crushed beneath a tire, and the child slipped out with all the glory of greasy entrails falling from a strung up quarry.

Olea hadn't seen the girl pass.

This was not her first midwifery. The initial seconds were the thing. She snipped mother from child like clipping a stem with a pair of sheers, separated the living from the dead, and tied him off.

Nobel watched as Olea wrapped their great-grandchild in a

cocoon of warm cotton, her arms and trunk covered in a lather of slaughter-tar and afterbirth.

The boy never cried.

He took his first breath in silence, and Nobel loved him straight away.

FOUR

Nobel was cobweb and muck covered.

He'd been replacing dry rot with new timber in the crawl beneath the house when Olea called out crow-like followed by the holler of a man Nobel didn't recognize. There wasn't a clean thing between the four of them, five if the deceased was counted. The young drifter who'd shepherded Ella to their hearth stood at the front door. The sun was at his back and shrouded his face. He was pole thin and a ruffian, Nobel discerned, and a .38 caliber handgun swung at his side like a headman's tool.

"Is he yours?" Nobel asked without releasing his granddaughter's fingers or looking from the boy's plum face.

"No." The word caught in the drifter's throat. "Don't know who's been made the proud father." He said and stepped inside.

The young man's jaw was thin and sprouted with tufts of hair that formed an unhealthy patchwork across his chin and neck. His head swayed to imagined music and his sockets had a hollow look. Drugs had taken a shovel to them and the lids retreated, pushing the black-spotted balls out like peas from a pod.

"She gone?" His voice was paper wrinkled.

"I'm afraid so." Nobel cradled his granddaughter's hand.

Olea eyed Ella's carcass and lost her breath.

"She had the AIDS and a habit." The drifter seemed to cough on his tongue. "Hep C too. As these things go, can't foresee little one will stay long."

Nobel recognized a conceit in the man that sparked his neck hairs.

"If the blood you're wearing finds a hole, you'll go with him." The drifter spread his feet to keep steady. "To wherever it is the accursed go."

He was at least a decade their granddaughter's senior but still a young man. His hands were grimy with torn nails, but vital. He wore a pinguid wool vest unbuttoned over a torn jersey camp shirt. His clothes were dusted gray and stiff as oilcloth from a road life but his mind kept its bite. Nobel knew his type, had crossed paths with his generational clone decade after decade and not once found him worthy of air.

"You made your way here, now find your way gone."

The young man's sedate smile spoke clearly. There would be no telling of how things are or what would be done unless he was doing so. He scratched at his bony thigh with the handgun's barrel to conclude his point.

"The folk that trade for newborns put a premium for white skin, should he live."

"You'll lay no hand on him." Olea said through her teeth.

"Go and fix me a meal and coddle me with that tenderness in a warm bath, old bird, and then we'll be leaving, that boy and I, with a week's supply."

He said it like it had already been done, Nobel thought, and cupped his granddaughter's palms on her belly.

Since boyhood he'd despised handguns. His mongrel Bill had picked up the enmity as is common in dogs with their masters. This one was Smith and Wesson and showed rust on its hammer. It could've spread to the latch pin. That would slow its response. Nobel had rifle hunt and brought down bird with buckshot, but killing a man with a firearm was cowardice. Handguns served no other purpose. This one's ejector rod was bent and corroded. The brass butts in its cylinder could be spent. Nobel couldn't make out the primer pockets.

"You're wondering if it'll fire. There are souls that could testify its capital, if they still lodged in the living."

Nobel's mutt was the son of a Chesapeake Bay Retriever and calf-sized sewer rat, Nobel had always said. He saw just the flash of Bill's yellow teeth. The man's scream was the only human sound as the dog grunted, shook its cinder block head and took three of the man's digits off with the stock of the pistol. Then there was only the drifter's wailing.

To survive a mortal length and never fight a man who needed beating, never breed a descendant better than you, never make a mistake large enough to leave a shadow, was that a lifespan worth the time it took? As a lawman Nobel had said this as his daily prayer, and did so until he'd conceded his judgeship and they'd moved off the grid. He was old, as good as sterile, and straw-stuffed at best. His bones were splintery calcifications and his head was a pebble burred by tubeworms and spiked on a neck bone that slung off his shoulders like a pumpjack. He needed a glass to read, his nails had submitted to fungus, and he couldn't climb a barn ladder without breaking for his heart. He was a tortoise stripped naked and crucified, he'd be the first to admit, and even so, he could still lift a cast iron pan and swing it hard enough to brain a man silent.

Their seven-fingered tormentor fell unnamed to the porch wood dead. His depressed skull filled a bowl of blood soup, and the boy hadn't made a sound.

FIVE

Olea brought the boy close to his mother as Nobel pulled the man down the back steps.

"Where are you taking that?"

If Nobel heard her over the din of forehead bone clapping on tread boards he didn't make it known. His slow going made his sounds of strain more unsettling. She knew he'd killed men before. It was a liability of his work, but that was long ago and never at home.

"Your not speaking of who she is only twists the knife in me."

"Let the parting have their silence," Nobel finally said. "The boy should know his mother before she cools."

The infant couldn't see like he would when fully formed. As a newborn, his sight was limited but Olea knew he could feel, and Nobel was right. Their granddaughter still had the warmth of life.

She nestled him in the cuddle of the girl's neck and bosom.

Fit for a portrait, she imagined, and bit her lip to slow its trembling.

There are religions that believe the soul remains in the body for a period after death. This would be the moment the boy would have beyond the womb with his mother. Olea would tell him about it one day and he'd know the comfort of having shared her this way. Perhaps the girl's soul might know this grace too, and hold it during eternity. Olea could hope, but nothing more.

She would have known her, even if the spindly doll hadn't whispered *Grandma* like a forbidden plea when she tripped at their stoop.

Her name was Ella, Olea recalled, and saw herself in the pieces of broken mirror the two made. The born and the passed, concentric ripples in a pond.

"Oh, child. What did we do?"

When an orphan couldn't be placed locally the county would open the door to greater populations. If she and Nobel refused her, the girl would get a life with young parents in a suburban environment, they'd decided. She'd have friends and maybe even siblings and grow up loved appropriately and surrounded by possibility. Olea could never see her, however, that was the arrangement. Ella's opportunities would be like wildflowers for her to pick, Nobel had said.

Olea cleared the strings of hair from her granddaughter's face and closed her eyes. She was a comely girl in spite of the injury done to her. Scars ran like a roadmap on her body. This was their legacy.

The boy lay quiet on her, head at his mother's chin, his arms reaching out slowly like branches brushing against her face and neck in their sway. This would be his only caress.

Olea felt tremors run through her and looked to the boy, as

if he could help her.

I'm a bird who's struck a window, that's all, she thought, and clutched the table to slow her breathing as she hung her head over their rendering of the Madonna.

She'd mistaken a reflection in the window for reality again, and behind it was an emptiness that would hold this too, she told herself.

"How is the child?" Nobel returned.

"One lives. One does not."

He saw she wanted to throw blame. He expelled a breath through his nostrils to loose the knot in his lungs and took the infant from his mother. As he handed the boy to Olea, Nobel felt his ribcage tighten like seismic plates and he kicked the chair from beneath the table. It righted with a clamor.

What were they? Two people entering their final years, with two dead bodies and a helpless newborn that would need milk soon.

"You closed her eyes."

"Did not. It was her ghost."

It was her way to spur him when off balance. He knew the alternative and appreciated her mettle.

She and the puckered baby stared at him with clouded eyes, the beginning and end of a story.

"He will survive just fine on goat's milk," Olea said, and that was the end of the discussion.

Nobel took his granddaughter into his arms. A hollow sack, she was lighter now.

This stuck him to the floor and her head fell back onto his shoulder. Her throat was clean and she slept on his nape as a child. He gripped her tight as the earthquake came and shook tears down the cliffs of his peach pit face.

SIX

The ground was hard as fired clay.

Each stroke of the shovel vibrated electricity through his skeleton like conduit to his strained muscles. He relished it. The sting in his skin from the sun and dust and black flies. The compressing of his back like his spine was a spike struck by a sledge. The grit rubbed into the wet beneath the torn peel of his palms. It all made the task easier. Olea had removed Ella's clothing. They'd laid her over a quilt on the flinty ground, and she cleaned her body now with a linen towel and warm water she'd dosed with lavender.

They had both read the tattoo on the girl's hand. *Remember always you are loved.*

It was in a script they knew. Olea in particular since she'd penned it. The scroll wrapped the belly of Ella's thumb, ending with *your Grandmother* and their postal address.

It had originally been a letter Olea'd written to her after her father's death, delivered by a childcare worker, evidently carried since and ultimately duplicated into her skin. That's how she and the drifter had found them.

Nobel knew his way around almost every criminal pursuit. He felt confident a man killed whose body was never found, and whose ending whereabouts and company were never known, was nothing more than a missed person. In this case who'd likely never be so. But who dropped them if they'd hitched? By the looks of their feet they'd walked their final miles. He would hike back to the road and see what signs they'd left. What sort of man or woman abandoned a girl in need on the side of the road, he wondered. It would take an unfeeling person, no matter her appearance or companion.

He'd pulled a circular cattle crib from the attic. Olea had made a shade with a parasol and the boy laid with them as they worked.

"If any of what took her is in him, we'll be back here soon."

"Is doubt to be your defining accomplishment?"

Nobel deserved the scolding, he thought, and squared the hole's corners as she washed their granddaughter's body of all blood and tarnish until only the tulip field of sores and bruising stained her girlish pallor.

Nobel climbed from the grave, sunk the shovel into the mound and watched Olea rinse Ella's hair in a fresh pail, dry it in her cotton skirt and weave in chicory flower and blue phlox. Then he spilt the roiled water and they each took a quilt corner, raised her up and lowered her down to her den of afterlife.

The infant's eyes struggled to discern, finding them at last with his ears, Nobel decided.

"Will you give her words, Judge?"

With his eyes on the dead, Nobel recited their goodbye.

"There has fallen a splendid tear, from the passion-flower at the gate.

She is coming, my dove, my dear; She is coming, my life, my fate; The red rose cries, 'She is near, she is near;' And the white rose weeps, 'She is late;' The larkspur listens, 'I hear, I hear;' And the lily whispers-"

Nobel said no more and Olea released a handful of soil into the hole, powdering the body's belly.

"I wait."

SEVEN

The young man deserved no such grave, Nobel thought, at least as he was no relation.

It seemed the only practical choice to section the remains into pieces comestible to the pigs. It was an unsettling task, but they'd benefit from the offspring it fostered.

If this is your only generosity, consider it a gift, Nobel said to the drifter, as he exsanguinated him over the trough.

Nobel hadn't found the gun. He'd looked for hours and decided Bill had buried it somewhere like he'd done with other favorite toys since a puppy. If the dog's artistry held, it would never be found, except perhaps as an artifact a thousand years from now when a new species greater than ours went digging in the caliche for explanations.

The trudge to the county highway was overgrown with bull thistle and beggars lice and if it hadn't just been trampled through he may not have found his way out, Nobel had to admit, and added a sense of direction to his growing list of degradations.

After a few hours search, he found a small pink valise in the cross vine off the road's shoulder, dried banana-like fruit pods clutching it like gritty hands.

Nobel walked two miles one direction and then the other and found the car. It was off the blacktop and backed into a nest of bramble, the hood topped in branches.

He was struck with the thought that he'd find the sedan's driver dead or injured inside but the interior and trunk were empty. Likely the pair had lifted it and stowed it here for their getaway. He popped the hood, pulled a hose from the radiator and syphoned off the end of the gas. Then he shook the hose clear, returned it and removed the branch-work. Joyriders ran it aground and walked away is what the law would think.

He wiped the inside and handles and covered any tracks their direction, and left the vehicle with the look of abandon to shore this up.

He did his best to restore the anonymity of the trail on his return, comforted that it was growing season and the underbrush wouldn't be denied any open ground.

They had a strong well, a climate forgiving enough they could grow their foodstuffs, and ample livestock to husbandry until their end. Unless a lightening strike burned them out, if they gave their health to nature, none of them need ever return this way. Until the boy outlived them, perhaps.

The small case contained Ella's lifetime of possessions. A partial stack of playing cards with photos of New Orleans on their backside, a dirty toothbrush, empty pill bottles, a dated video camera, rusty utility knife, sullied underthings, a moth bit cardigan, half a Bible with burnt page edges, a hair comb, a quarter roll of toilet paper, an empty lighter, a drug cooking spoon bent for convenience, and a pink-haired doll meant for a schoolgirl, covered in grease mars and dried mud. The toy looked like it had been towed behind a coal train.

Olea cleaned it all, leaving no item loathed. She straightened and polished the spoon, repaired the tears, and shined the flaked clasps, handle and hardware of the case.

Inside the video camera was a cassette.

Neither was stirred to see what was on it just yet. It would be a year before they gave it audience. For now, Nobel neatly repacked the case and put it in the back of the storage closet in their study. It was the boy's inheritance.

Nobel cut a hole in an old ketchup cap, fashioned a nipple from a rubber thimble and secured both to the bottle. After some effort Olea was able to nurse the boy with milk warm from the goat.

The last time they'd been here had ended badly, but Olea had a glow that said she'd hungered for absolution longer than he'd known.

The boy would be their providence.

Their failure had left a second chance in a basket at their door.

EIGHT

Present day

She could hear his mumbled gibberish from the kitchen as he repeated the tape's final moment again and again and drank himself into a stupor, and she felt the unpleasantness of being alone, for the first time since they'd abandoned the rest of the world.

They were in the low mountains of southern Missouri, remote to begin with and urban resettlement trends would make it more so. She'd chosen their specific property because it was vast and set off from any meaningful throughway. The one dirt road in was practically invisible and impassable now. A black walnut and a loblolly had fallen across it and she'd had Nobel leave them to rot beneath the wild growth. The trailhead off the highway was a difficult plod that seemed without purpose and she'd made sure it couldn't be seen from the asphalt. The only sign of habitation was a postal stake at the roadside the carrier used to drop letters and supplies in a wooden box with a flag for outgoings that moss had covered. She'd set up a trust with Nobel's retirement to pay their taxes in perpetuity. If they had a need they couldn't meet themselves, she parceled it via a letter to her sister, collect on delivery.

Was this one of those times, she asked herself as she snuck downstairs. She wrapped the boy in a blanket and took him in her arms on the floor. How Nobel had gone cold to the child eluded her. She could hear him upstairs wrestling scripture. She'd chosen isolation to shake off the fester and it had wormed into her final human bonds.

The boy shuffled and she tried to clear her mind.

His breathing was steady against her and warmed her shawl. His severed wrist had already scabbed. So there was no need to dress it. She could see his face twitch, as if with content visions as he dreamt in unspoiled security. She hummed a cradlesong and swayed them to its measure to drown out Nobel's doubt.

In the light wash of the television, Nobel pitched in his rocker, staring at the walls, and imagined the comfort of iron bars that he couldn't escape. The chair's joints shrieked like breaking tree limbs but his doweled frame was sturdy and at ease, he thought, and felt a cold walk through him.

A spectral unknown shook the fungus and warts from his fringes, and freed his calcified neck to spire straight on his steely spine, he shouted, mimicking a carnival barker, touting a creature from another planet.

The miracle-wielding snake handlers of his youth were men who'd replaced reason with a single passage of the New Testament. In hindsight they'd hid beneath sheets of deception, pretending to be ghosts. The only power of God they had touched was hubris. He'd been baptized Pentecostal but had no say in it, so was born again as a married man, inducted into the church that had turned Olea into a teetotaler. It wasn't unusual to desire faith. He knew he'd embraced it more with age, as the sand he cupped in his hands slipped away.

Is each man every man's protector or is that God's work alone, he asked the ether, and swallowed the end of his jar of hooch.

What had his father said? *A worthless dish you were named after, but this one's filled with magic*, and then he'd slide an empty glass vessel across the table where it would catch in his birthday cake's frosting. He said it each year and every time believed it was a first, until Nobel had five containers of certified enchantment, sealed beneath an airtight lid. Over his lifetime, in outbursts of nostalgia or pleas for divination, Nobel had opened each one and waited for the magic to cure him, and each became a worthless jar again. The one he held was the survivor. He blew a puff of rancid air into it, sealed the cap and stared into the glass like a crystal ball.

Was he slipping into delusion, without knowing it? Wasn't that part of delusion?

"And they brought unto him all sick people that were taken with diverse diseases and torments, and those which were possessed with devils, and those which were lunatic," he hollered, and tried to stand to get closer to the television but got vertigo and sat again.

He watched his hands shake like an epileptic, barely able to keep his head from resting in his lap. Did they need the boy like a junkie needed heroin?

Olea kept a framed photograph in the foyer, of Cole as a boy standing beside Nobel in his County uniform. It was conspicuous to Nobel's every move. He could see it now like a signal fire and threw himself forward, and made it to his feet this time.

"Prepare slaughter for his sons because of the guilt of their fathers, lest they rise and possess the earth!" He braced the wall and put his face to the picture glass. *"This, our son, is stubborn and rebellious. He will not obey our voice. He is a glutton, and a drunkard,"* Nobel spoke and

caught his eyes in the reflection. *"And all the men of his city shall stone him with stones, that he die."*

Was this cabin fever, or was the vine of evil first an innocuous root that begged to be ripped out before it sprouted and went to seed? Leviticus warned of magic and those who claimed its deliverance, but wasn't the greater threat those who would seek to exploit it?

So we were to kill the magic among us for our protection, not because it was damned itself but to save it from evil hands.

Can one man be that judge? He whispered and fell back into the cradle of his chair's arms.

The boy couldn't exist, without everything a human being ever built or believed skewing into an Escherian stairwell. They'd kept him to settle their own failed duty. That was the truth not being spoken. Their motive was selfish.

The boy was a gift they hadn't the grace to decline, and there was no one to save them from themselves.

Nobel fell still for a moment. The world seemed to hold time for him.

What if the devil, apocryphal or parable or as real as the boy appeared, what if he offered up a second apple?

Hadn't the hand of nature attempted to pluck him from them, and they'd fought it back.

NINE

Six years ago
___

Nobel could see the boy from where he stood, playing in the corner with whittled toys.

The child had followed him, gosling to his gander since the day he could walk.

Whether milking goats, hog slaughter or farriery, he was a watchful appendage at Nobel's side. He'd ride in the saddle with Nobel to tend their small crop of corn, wheat and alfalfa. He kept an eye on every chore and was fast to help to the limits of his size and balance. Together they mucked out the stalls, fed the stock, pressed the grains for oil, tarred the roofs, mended fences, cared for the pumps and firewood and seed saving, and tilled and irrigated the fields.

When not with Nobel, the boy was at Olea's side, his hand in hers if it were free. Whether tending to the home, grooming the animals, planting and harvesting the garden and greenhouse, canning, sewing, cooking, pickling, or grinding their corn or grain, if the boy was near he had a hand on her. There was no aspect to their homestead life not improved because of the child. The way Olea brightened each day, he knew she felt the same. Even sleep mirrored their days in pleasant dreams.

Nobel rose, kissed her forehead and caught the air of sage on her skin. The boy stood with him. Nobel didn't bother looking back as he exited. The boy would be there.

The sun threw shadows like dark taffy pulled over the earth's edge. Their three horses were huddled, skittish at the fence. Dusk did that to the animals at times. Where was the dog though? The quiet at the barn made him stop. The boy heeled. Together they stood audience to horror as the large cat drug poor old Bill by the head, his intestines unwinding like a tale of jellyfish. There'd been a struggle, he was a stout mutt, but victory too often went to the aggressor who stole surprise.

Neck broke, legs convulsing, he was alive but would be done soon. A cougar that big could down a cow. It wouldn't raise a pulse disemboweling an old man and child. Their only advantage was the cat was in their gaze, but it wouldn't hold. A soundless hunter Nobel knew the mountain lion preferred to remain invisible until it struck from behind and crushed the spine at the head, paralyzing a prey to be carried off alive to a place safe for dining.

"Step back. Slowly, boy." Nobel knew the boy sensed the fear in his voice.

They both saw how curious the male cat stood, head drooped over their dying dog, its cheeks bathed in a slop of blood, eyes unblinking. It was a statue of predatory supremacy. They were being mesmerized, Nobel thought, and the hex broke when a shadow grabbed the boy by the head and leapt to the stable fence and feed shed.

The female cat made no sound to explain taking the child. It was not unheard of to find mountain lion in their parts. It was unearthly rare to witness a breeding pair at hunt in congress. The boy was limp in her jaws, arms and legs lifeless cloth in the breeze, a marionette with cut strings. The cat's fang had popped through an eyelid but the socket held. The boy's skull bones endured as far as Nobel could see. A red flow sheened his hair and the boy's lasting eye fixed on Nobel, unmoved. The wind stole two of his loves into the fire like dried leaves, so was the speed of it. The boy blinked, alive.

Nobel's head fell back, his throat caverned and he wailed like a stabbed mule, and lashed his arms against the air, a man insane. His lungs blew trumpets of agony and an orchestra of loss birthed from his belly as he stomped and hit the earth with his palms. Unknowable sounds spurt from him. He thrashed and keened, a shark thrown to the ground gnashing at the fiends, slapping the clay with his forearms and feet, his jaw unhinged and teeth clapping between yelps. There was no pretense. It was as unthinking as his heartbeat. This was how he reacted to a calamity of this kind. He saw himself from the outside, warped and rangy and frail, his body railing on the chert, still a man.

If the female fled, she'd disappear into the dark with the boy. There'd be no finding them. In daylight, Nobel would track her footsteps to a child's gutted cavity, the fat and flesh of the boy's face and small limbs cleaned to bone, his belly skin ripped off and ribs emptied of his heart, lungs, kidneys and liver, his waste organs in his lap like a gutted fish, his carcass a skeletal doll of meat slops thinly buried, dusted with her futile kicks of earthen crust to fend off the carrion eaters. Anguish poured out of Nobel in an impossible way and escalated still. He hadn't known his depth of feeling for the boy.

Olea rushed from their portico, called by the shrieks, a pot in each hand like a mad circus performer banging and screeching in a vibrato trill only primitive throats can reach. They were an elderly, bodily helpless couple rasping the darkness. Everything burst and they fought for their offspring and life itself against a younger, stronger couple yet to bear. Their livestock roiled, echoing their cries, and at the foray's crest the dog bayed his final rattle and the giant cats dropped their catch and flew into the night's blanket.

As mother and father Nobel and Olea took hold of the boy and knelt, Bill's animal form spiritless beside them, blood shared among all.

The boy gaped at them through his open eye, panting like a smote fledgling.

TEN

By candlelight they nursed their child.

Nobel had seen the cat shake the boy and feared his stem was snapped. He lay dormant on the same table he was born on.

Olea cleaned the squashed grape within his left eye socket and covered it with a sterile cloth.

Nobel pulled apart an apple box as she sewed the boy's scalp, closing his exposed skull. He splint the boy's spine with the box parts, as she dabbed on their antiseptics, dressed the wounds with honey and swaddled the boy with scraps of sheet.

The boy respired between them but was otherwise a lifeless toy painted with a blackface of gore. Nobel longed to break a piece of himself off to save the child but their job was done and nothing was left but vigilance and prayer.

They slept little, taking turns listening to the boy's breath and feeling his skin for fever. When the sun woke, so did the boy as if it was all a fiction.

"Momma? Papa? Why do you look afraid?"

It was a question Nobel wouldn't forget.

He washed and buried Bill in the family plot because he was kin.

The mutt had gotten old and his weakened senses had invited nature to consume him. He knew the dog had cleared a path he had no choice but to follow. How had the boy become so important? Was it a prank of God to give the soon to depart a reminder of life's splendor? Or was it just that joke eventually played on us all by the passing seasons? Nobel had been ten times the man he was now, yet before the child had never felt the desperation that infers real love. Was it the nakedness of old age that made appreciation possible at last? What of their boy, Cole? Had a demon rather than his own weakness swept him away, would their shells have crumbled to reveal their earliest need?

Within a week the boy seemed as well as before the mauling. They cut away the cotton strands and stitches and where there should have been a mark for his lifetime was clear. They removed the bandage from his left orbit soon after and found the eyeball returned in shape yet still ruddy and opaque, but in time the eye came to see again.

The boy's person was repaired in full.

He'd lived through a devouring and he was as good and original as born. Nobel's dog had died with and by God and earth. The boy survived by something else. How could it be? Something greater than a commitment to rapture kept the boy alive and restored him whole, something that renounced the laws of nature as well. He and Olea needed the boy to live on, not to be proclaimed aberrant.

Had their primeval petitions conjured this, Nobel asked himself, and weren't they now shepherding turpitude?

Olea had begged him to leave civilization to escape the unraveling, only to find its undoing in the child at her breast.

ELEVEN

Seventy-one years ago
___

Is it a sin to never trust your father?

To have no memory of feeling safe with him or at home yet no early incident to prove your presentiment, it was a heavy weight to grow up beneath, Nobel thought.

In the month of August, the bus from Houston to Kansas City started kiln dry and ended in boiled molasses. The driver had been a woman during the war, but since it ended young Mason Nobel had seen a man take the job. He preferred the woman. She smiled more, and took notice that he wasn't old enough to ride alone but did so anyway twice a year. The man didn't look at him at all. In fact he didn't look at anyone except the young women thin enough to show their knees beneath their skirt hems when they sat, particularly if they crossed their legs without modesty.

Nobel had learned a good deal about the nature of people on these trips to and from his grandparents and his birth home in Missouri. Middle-aged women, talking of who'd been to church with clenched teeth, determined to touch his dimples and crimp his cheeks. Nervous Chinese families with their dried fish and strange smelling provisions, always offering him rice candy. A large, suited gentleman with dark brown hair sticking out the back of his collar once put his puffy hand on Nobel at the crease of his thigh and left it there even when Nobel began to squirm. It was night and few passengers were awake. The man's head turned slow like a wind vane and stopped. His unblinking eyes moved the hand north. Something about the gorilla strength of it stunned Nobel, and he urinated. It wasn't deliberate but the man stood up just the same, wiped his hand on the seatback and walked the aisle to stretch his joints. When he returned he sat beside an elderly woman. Nobel preferred the sunlit hours after that. The night conceded its secrets too easily.

It wasn't his first battle scar. He'd had an uncle try a similar move years before. A few of the boys had divulged tales of lechers. Huddled around a campfire one in particular, Chip Carlyle, had told the whole pack about biting a man on the part of his person never meant to be shown. Chip had impressed them all with his confidence and it was his bravado Nobel beckoned when he chomped a piece off his uncle's thumb as he tried to slide it into his mouth like a straw.

It was a world of predator and game his father had said, when they'd went mule deer hunting and the younger kids had cried over the wheezing of a lung-shot goner. He'd said it with a confusing pride, Nobel recalled.

To pass the time on the bus, he'd empty his duffle and refold and stack each article, including his comics and undergarments, attempting to perfect the alignment. It was an activity that was comforting to him still. He could only do so if he sat alone or beside a heavy sleeper. His favorites would nip a flask until they passed out and their lap became a tabletop that stirred only when they spluttered on a clogged breath. These bus rides were his fondest childhood memories and where he created his foundation of security, he would later tell Olea.

The car ride from the Kansas City station to their home was better in the summer. Nobel would put his window down and hang out if his father drove. His mother believed that leaving a seated posture was unsafe. The ride this time wasn't to be what he thought.

His father had been away because of the war. He was a peace officer prior to conscription, served his duty as military police before discharge and came home with a taste for brandy and no use for servitude. Nobel knew him as the manager of the downtown hardware exchange. Their car was old and he could recognize the sound before he saw it. When he got in, he habitually centered his feet on the Linoleum tiles that covered the rust holes in the floorboards before closing the door. The struts snapped and popped, the frame threatened to bottom-out on every bump like a boat in a creek, and the interior smelled like someone spilt fry grease into an ashtray.

His father clutched the wheel two-handed. His shiny skin gathered around his mouth like a prune around its pit and he chewed on his own cheek like tobacco. Nobel noticed his knuckles were swollen and lacerated and he was unshaven, but hadn't grown enough grass to cover the scratch on his neck. At each stop he'd turn to stare at Nobel as if with something to say, but without the nerve to pick a word. It was a look Nobel would see a thousand times on men and women in his career. He leaned against the door and stuck his head into the wind, and his father pulled him back so fiercely he almost emptied his bowels on the vinyl.

He was a sensitive child, the doctors had said. Nobel'd

done his best to thicken his skin but his emotions were often faster than his awareness of them. He hadn't been overcome in years, shivered at the thought, and studied his father to see what was to come as they drove. He'd had friends with fathers whose temper would color them in ways only the most creative painter could duplicate. Nobel's father had always kept his rage capped. Where it poured safely out, Nobel didn't know.

His father guided him to enter the house first, which hadn't happened before. That was how Nobel remembered him, standing at the sidewalk, pacing back and forth like a streetwalker, as if he wasn't permitted on his own lawn. Inside he found his father's still wet artwork on his Mother's face and arms. A Monet might have flowered her back and chest in red and blue as well, but her dress and smock hid it.

Her voice quavered when she spoke but she stood tall and never broke his stare. "Your father is gone, Mason. He is not your father no more."

There were stains on the carpet that had only just started to brown. "What did he do? Did he make those marks on you?"

"This isn't a time for questions. You're grown today"

Nobel's younger sister had been born with palsy and his mother had coddled her and raised him to man the home. He thought this was the surprise he sensed coming. From the moment he'd got into his father's car without as much as a wink or look in the eye, he felt the jack-in-the-box of his life cranking. His mother's mosaic of contusions had shocked him but they were just the shudders foretelling the eruption. The jester didn't pop from the box, however, he stepped from the bedroom meant to belong to the husband. Nobel's Mother introduced him as Byron. His skin was as dark as cola and he was equal in height and width to the upright Kodiak grizzly they'd seen at the Natural History Museum in Chicago, and talked as much.

"Who's he to be?" Nobel whispered.

"He's to care for your mother. You're to be the man of the house."

Byron stayed good to his mother and sister and gave Nobel the sort of securing presence the earth did the moon, and he never saw his father again except as occasion took him to need hardware. To this day Nobel believed the best man he'd ever met was the bear that took his mother to bed.

At sixteen Nobel came home to his mother frightened and fighting tears. A police officer friend of his father's stood behind her like a shadow. Byron had been found, rope bound to each limb, she said between tremors, torn into parts by the heave of two tractors.

That's what it would take, Nobel later told people, and recollected his cheeks wetting and the floor giving like the planet was an egg hollowed out.

Proud drunks gabbed for years of the black bear man getting his due, and whispered tales of Nobel's father at the helm of the pull. The image etched into Nobel like he'd been there too, but he never faced his father about it, he later told Olea, and didn't attend the funeral when he was found dead twenty-years after, alone on his knees before a Bible dosed in his urine, his liver soaked to pungency.

Nobel spent more time surveying these events and their ricochets than any others. No road map ever revealed itself. In fact within a few decades he remembered little at all. It became a habit of his brain to lose track of his own story, and he used the extra space for things that mattered, he'd say when pressed.

The only memory he had that held a flare was a time he'd opened his mother's door without knocking, and had seen Byron's back. It brought Jackson Pollock's *Blue Poles* to mind, and clearly took years and multiple artists to complete.

Byron didn't say a word. He just set a hand on Nobel's shoulder from his Kodiak height, and Nobel felt like he couldn't fall, because a man held him. That's the only way he could describe it. For a moment, he didn't have to climb, because he was the mountain.

Nobel had read enough as an adult to know he had torn and stolen pages in his early chapters but no person or scripture could tell him how to correct or retrieve them.

His solace was that he'd been the best husband-child he could be, and though his mother had passed over forty years ago, he still was.

TWELVE

Three years ago

_____

Gone to town. Whatever it is we want nothing of it.

The sign was old. Handwritten on a scrap of fabric and strung over the window of the front door. It was hard to say if its aged appearance implied the author had since departed or its continued reuse.

The man at the door knew he was just a messenger of the court and had already outdone his duty spelunking the cavern of thorny weeds and fallen trees that once was the road in. The place appeared to be a survivalist's homestead. His chore was simply delivery of notice. He pounded the door again. The porch was swept, the windows not opaque with grime. There were residents. The land of the homesteaders was large. The fields expanded beyond the barn, and wooded valleys and hills surrounded them to the horizon. He'd seen it on the map. It was too much to scavenge. There could be a dozen other farmhouses in other clearings unknown to surveyors. An aerial drafting hadn't been done in twenty years.

"Hello? Mr. Nobel? Mrs. Nobel?" He paused as long as seemed fit then walked the circumference. Each window revealed no party. "Mr. Mason Nobel? Mrs. Olea Nobel? Is there a person present to stand as representative?"

The boy had spotted him working through the weave that covered their drive. The thought of coming so far just to go back unappeased was the only thing that could've kept the man from giving up, Nobel decided. There was no other logical reason to endure the trek in, particularly in his getup. If he entered the home without being invited Nobel could shoot him and be within his rights. It was not his first choice.

The boy liked the appearance of the man. He wore spectacles that he'd never seen. The glass was dark and hid his eyes. They made him look supernatural. He also wore a suit like the boy had only seen in magazine photos and those of Nobel's wedding. It was burr covered but still made an impression, he thought.

They were huddled in the root cellar beneath the home's floor, careful not to be spotted through the two half windows. It was nothing but damp storage still and adults had to hunch to stand.

The man outside stopped before the back mudroom door. The porch wrapped the house and he could see three thin horses grazing from where he stood. It was likely he'd get himself a faceful of buckshot if he stuck his nose any further inside private thresholds. This wasn't his first backward Missourian.

"Hello?! Is there anyone about?!"

The old couple could have passed away years ago. A den of methamphetamine industrialists might be behind the walls, or even beneath the floors. A squat of twitching psychopaths could be huddled below his feet that very second, with their guns aimed straight at his privates. There was no evidence of it, but he was alone and carried no weapon because his duty required none. His job was done if he posted the notice, properly taped to the front door. So he did so and departed.

Once they caught site of him reentering the labyrinth of bristle, Olea went up first. Nobel watched her march upstairs while his feet held to the dry mud, unwilling to part. She'd say the testosterone trade of aging had finally weighed in her favor. The truth was Nobel had been incapacitated by the thought of having to kill a man, because the world was a threat to the boy, not because the man threatened their immediate lives. So he was waiting for his target to get further away.

The boy had a book in hand and a question in tow. He knew who was the more interested party when it came to the stories he read or he'd be holding Olea's skirt, proving himself a braver soldier as well.

"Are their people still kept as slaves in the world?"

"There are but it is not the same."

Nobel saw Olea moving for higher ground to track the man by the wag of the sapling tops and mounted the steps. The boy followed.

"Why don't you and momma do something for them?"

"The older you get the more disappointment you store in your belly, and the bigger your belly gets the less tolerant you are of having it exposed."

Nobel watched the boy raise his brow, trying to understand.

"What's less tolerant?"

"As it pertains to your topic? The circle of what a person believes they can affect shrinking over time. It starts as the universe and ends as the thoughts in your head."

"Do you talk like that to stop me from asking questions?"

"Every man is a slave to something, child. It's his charge to free himself or choose a master more wisely."

Nobel pulled the delivered notice from the door jam and opened it.

"That's why you don't do anything?"

"We thought about joining an international organization, and decided living here and caring for you was better."

It was a county document, officiating a statement of will and testament.

"What about New York City? Are there cities with so many people?"

"You're reading books. That doesn't make the places real."

"I know. That's why I'm asking you."

"You know momma and I love you."

"You always say that when you want me to stop talking."

"So do as you know I'm wanting."

"Okay, Papa."

Nobel's sister had passed. The sum total of her worth and adjunct of insurance was his to have, if he'd claim it with his signature, or it would be surrendered to the descendants of her husband departed. She'd found love in a blind man. A fellow Nobel favored, he recalled, who had died before his time. She'd never had children, fearing that she'd pass on her imperfection or his. Nobel hadn't seen her in twenty-two years. He knew her end days were spent solitary, in a one-room apartment, just like their mother.

The boy saw Nobel's grief before Nobel felt it himself, and put a hand around Nobel's thumb and finger and squeezed. Another scourge of getting old, Nobel thought. The past didn't just pull you back, it plunged you like a river baptism, and the further back you went the deeper the drowning.

The buzzing caught Nobel's attention before his heart sank. It was the deceptive sort, a loud sound made faint by distance.

Olea came to the porch. She still had topsoil from the back garden on her sandals. From the rise she'd watched the stalks swish until she knew the man was gone.

She said nothing, but Nobel knew he should come outside.

THIRTEEN

It was an engine in the sky.

It began to hiccup like an instrument missing a stroke. Theirs was the only open land for miles so it was not pure chance the plane had found them. There was no primitive way to hide from the firmament.

He saddled his younger mare and kicked her toward the fields. The small plane had circled. He knew the variety and had been inside a few. The coughing smoke said it would soon succumb to the planet's tug. The unknown was the pilot's skill.

The corn had not yet been harvested, but the land lay flat. The green stalks bowed like hair parting in the wind and the wheat was still young stubble. Nobel had filled his rifle before mounting. His hands felt like skin stretched over a coat hanger in the reigns, and his horse was old and short but had pluck. He surfed the wave of her gallop to keep his bones from breaking like china in a sack.

The machine fell with talent. Nobel had missed birds with shot and seen a clipped-wing come down. This one was as elegant, with the looming violence of two thousand pounds of metal crumpling as it struck ground.

The plane was small but could have two passengers or more, or a substantial cargo.

It spiraled for their flats.

This was how it always happened, Nobel thought. One insurmountable difficulty immediately topped by another. That was his life. Didn't the boy prove that?

It was hard to say if the plane's clamor and trail would draw notice. The court appointed deliveryman would be nearing his vehicle and the trees would make it impossible for him to see the plane, which could just be passing over. Their closest neighbor was twenty miles off. The land that abutted theirs was private and wild, but could hide a random witness. The nation of his youth had gotten so crowded even their middling hills that secreted no ore or big game, but concealed them, still weren't remote enough to disappear in completely. The death of anonymity was the legacy of advance and it was a loss only those who knew it well would mourn.

It occurred to Nobel as he rode beneath the fuselage that it could hold a family, a young pilot perhaps with an infant sitting on his young wife's lap. Good people who travelled by aircraft the way others did by car.

Confinement sickness had turned everything into a menace, but more than just their lives were at stake if the boy was discovered, and his scanner was working. It had a thirty-mile range and had been powered since they'd decamped. If these visitors had called for help he would've known. Radio silence meant they considered announcing their presence a greater danger than gravity. Didn't it?

Nobel kicked his heels.

The pilot rode the late model Cessna like he was in a children's book strapped to a dying pterodactyl, but if he kept his nerve they'd beat the treetops and make his pastures.

Sure enough, the pilot used his engine's last pull to make the turn and clipped the crowns of pumpkin ash, slipped as if the air was a trip hazard and cuffed Nobel's wheat like a stone skipped across a millpond. Nobel booted his nag to meet their stop but couldn't keep their pace.

It was hard to imagine anything surviving the final somersaults the plane took as both wings were shed and all its glass shattered.

Nobel slowed as he neared the capsule. He could see the shape of a man hanging downward, moving where the copilot sat. The figure tended to the man trapped in the pilot seat then turned to face Nobel and his horse.

Nobel realized he had a rifle conspicuously strung to his back.

The copilot for now was the healthier of the two, Nobel surmised, and the pilot pointed an H and K MP7 at him and squeezed off a spray.

Nobel's mare spared him with her thick neck and skull.

The bullets hit the lung and missed her heart so she fell slow and Nobel got his leg out before her weight flattened the ground.

Nobel threw his rifle barrel over the mare's ribcage and got a shot off that grazed the copilot and struck the face of the gunman.

The gunfire echoed against the hills.

Even if that notice carrier hadn't felt it worth the abrasions to investigate the sound of the plane, he'd definitely return to his office and send others now, wouldn't he? The frustration of his slog could have numbed him to any new calls for attention, or he might be driving away and just imagine hillbillies shooting the sky to celebrate his hoodwinking.

The copilot was scrambling for the pilot's weapon.

Nobel's horse was dead. He was in a stony pinch.

FOURTEEN

Present Day

Nobel woke with a drool slick on his sternum and chalk jacket on his tongue.

Olea was looking at him from the door. The boy stood at her side, his surviving fingers in hers. The lunacy of the night was gone, but lucidity had not replaced it. Was his mania circling his crippled sanity from the shadows, a hyena waiting for it to die?

Sight of the one-handed child made Nobel's stomach roll. Only a monster did such a thing. The silence said the generator had run its tank dry. It was knowledge that infected him. If he could just imagine it away or bury it somewhere inside him, to fester in the dark of his subconscious, and resist its fever until it died with him. The truth tormented far more than a lie ever could.

Nobel's frame felt sturdier than it had been in twenty years. Hadn't he been strong enough to drag the boy?

He stared at the two of them, beldam and amputee. The

way they hung their eyes in the morning drear recalled a Lempicka painting he'd seen. *The Refugees* it was called. Maybe he could head the house for more years. Maybe the boy would grow slighter than his chassis suggested. He was a sensitive stripling and might not gain the will to defy.

Was hope the wire they waddled above the abyss?

Nobel stood. He expected the boy to flinch but he didn't. Instead he stared like a demiurge, hypnotized by the mystery of suffering. As Nobel stepped closer, he noticed the boy's lip quivering, and scorned the conceit of this thought.

The brown of the boy's blood was on his garments and dried into mud on his cheeks where his tears had puddled. The marquees of invisible scars he'd marked the boy with, they advertised a movie that would play on inside him long after he was washed. Nobel knew this secret theater, the unconscious mind locked forever in audience of a film that never changed, regardless of the choices we made or placards we chose.

"If only Norman Rockwell were alive to sketch us," Olea said without humor.

Nobel knelt to the floor.

"You don't feel discomforted?" The boy's stump had a cap of hard scab, and although sensitive to contact didn't give him hurt.

"No, Papa."

He could be lying, fearing another act of hysteria, or he could be trying to stave off Nobel's regret.

There was no denying he was an intelligent child. His soul was uncorrupted. It was something else that held the boy, and remained in him. No matter what Nobel cut away it would only grow, yearning like fruit to be swallowed by a creature that might defecate its seeds among the unknowing.

Nobel found Olea's eyes and they said she knew he was

fighting madness. Had he seen too much in his life? Maybe this was all taking place in his mind.

"Take the child and do your dailies," she said and then kissed the boy on the forehead and left him staring at Nobel.

"I am sorry, boy. I will not hurt you again." The boy didn't move. "Let's do our duty to the home together."

Nobel stood up and eyed the child.

He couldn't know if the boy chose to obey whether that would mean he'd been convinced, or if his empathy for Nobel had simply proven more powerful than self-preservation. Compassion was the key evil used to steal innocence from the good.

"Will you join me now?"

Nobel paused, wondering if the thing inside the boy sensed his fear and then went to the kitchen, splashed water on his face and neck and exited. The boy followed.

Together they cleared the stables and Nobel watched as the boy checked the abdomen and manure of their still gangling foal and rubbed its neck and snout with only one hand.

It wasn't more than a week before the skin had grown back over the boy's stubbed forearm.

In another ten-day's time the nubs of new fingers showed their sprouts like pink seedlings with tiny nails.

By two month's time the boy's full arm and hand had grown, returned like a salamander's tale, just as Nobel knew it would.

FIFTEEN

Three years ago
___

Nobel had the advantage.

They had superior weaponry but he had a safe position and was not currently strung upside down in an aircraft.

He snorted and caught the stink of blood. He assumed it was the mare's then felt a sting at his kidney. There was a red spurt there. It was standard for their firearm to tube armor piercing rounds. The projectile must have penetrated through his stepper's chest bone, throat muscle and mane with enough kinetic power to still breach his body. He felt his lower back and found the exit. Being thin had its advantages in a gunfight. How fast his wound would incapacitate him was the question.

Olea must have heard the shots. Would she decide to arm herself and the boy and barricade the house or suss out this Mexican standoff, between two failing parties and the patience of death.

To be armed as they were, the aircraft had to hold a stow of drugs, contraband or money. If they were heading south it would be money, north one of the other. None of which did them any good. They could use paper currency to kindle their fires. A small amount of narcotics would be useful but the rest would just dissolve in the plane when the rains came. He'd expected the worst but never contemplated this wretched a pickle.

He didn't have a good shot from where the horse fell, but if they tried to escape the plane he'd be able to clip them easily enough. He could smell the petrol but fuel rarely ignited. Perhaps one of them would be a pathetically addicted smoker and flamboyantly toss a match, Nobel imagined and laughed aloud. Humor struck him at the most inopportune times, he thought, and pinched his side.

He wasted a few rounds attempting to hit metal near the leaking tank and gave up to conserve his munitions. There was no other cover nearby and he was slow. It wouldn't take more than a blind man shooting toward the sound of his footsteps with that weapon to drop him before he reached the nearest grove.

His dead horse's bowels and bladder suddenly released with a trumpet of flatulence, and he laughed again. The two men listening must think he's a madman.

The odor was rotten. The manure mixed with the urine and horse blood flowed along his side. Just bad luck, his location, holed in behind the haunches.

He could hear them talking but it was garbled, maybe because of their distance or because it wasn't his native tongue.

"Do you two speak English? If you do, give me a reason not to toss this grenade under your heads."

It was a bluff but they couldn't know that. Nobel waited, counting turkey vulture orbits and reached seventeen.

"We would like to make a deal with you, viejo."

The voice was intelligible but slurred by a Spanish accent, Mexican or El Salvadorian maybe.

"We are going to try to get out of this plane. If you shoot at us we will not only kill you, but any family and animals you have back at that house and barn. We will burn one limb at a time in front of you." The pilot shouted this without appearing distressed.

Nobel had never liked being threatened. He realized no one enjoyed it but it had a history of creating irrational behavior in him. The wisdom of knowing so had yet to deter it. Like a fitful monkey he palmed up a fistful of manure, soil and equine blood and threw it toward the plane. It struck the fuselage near the copilot and splattered.

"You think I won't blow up your plane because I want what's inside it with you. I don't. You're worried about running out of ammo, blood or both. I'm not. If I decide you're not worth wasting ordnance on, I'll just wait all night for you to die. I brought a sandwich."

The men in the plane paused, and then began to laugh. Nobel chuckled with them. It wasn't without camaraderie.

"I was a lawman. I know you're not travelling south with medical supplies to save the sick and orphaned."

"The direction we are travelling is not your business," shouted the copilot. His voice surged like an out of tune pipe organ. An abdominal injury was the likely cause.

"I'll give you one more chance. La ultima! Why shouldn't I let this grenade burst you like human piñatas and spread your assholes over my wheat field?"

Nobel could hear the men talking again but couldn't make out their words. They had likely radioed someone of their descent with a satellite phone of some kind. An outfit like theirs would be well funded and wouldn't travel without a backup plan. Only dementia or unbridled narcissism could have kept them from understanding their odds. They would've transmitted his coordinates. If they hadn't, their own families and prized animals would be creatively slaughtered, whether they survived or not. That's how their loyalty was guaranteed.

He had to know whom they'd told of him before they died.

"When's your cavalry coming?" Neither of the trapped men made a sound. "The answer's not in time."

If the organization they worked for had his longitudinal and latitudinal location Nobel couldn't hide. He, Olea and the boy would have to move and there was no doing that. They'd all have to take the road of Zimri. There'd be no other escape. This was getting worse by the second. If the two men expired before he could confirm who might be arriving after them, he'd have no peace again even in death.

Maybe they weren't as sophisticated an outfit. It wasn't a modern plane and there were only two of them. Perhaps they relied on cellular telephones, which he knew for a fact to be ineffective at their current point.

"My wife was a nurse and did a military tour in Korea. She will be able to save you, if you're able to be saved." This wasn't true either, but she had been a nurse and midwife and Nobel hoped to glean what he needed before Olea laid eyes on them.

"We would like your wife's assistance." The copilot called out.

It suddenly occurred to Nobel that they could have a tracking device hidden within their cargo. It had become popular among criminals in the past decades. If he got to it, that could be their rescue. Any mercenaries to come would lose interest in the early whereabouts of whatever was in that plane, once they'd retrieved it. For all they'd know, these two packed it out, and then lost it to whomever Nobel could get to transport the payload far from where it was now. Of course, he had to do all of this before bleeding out.

"We will throw out our weapon. You may then take us to your wife."

Nobel didn't respond. Their injuries were the mortal sort or they were being duplicitous.

He saw the flash of metal and could hear the heavy thud of the submachine gun as it landed on the lea between them. The odds they had only that single weapon were slim, particularly given its gusto. They would have a handgun as sidekick, at the very least.

As he thought this, a second object lofted from the cabin and landed between him and the MP7.

It was a .45 caliber Colt automatic pistol with a gold-plated grip, stuck in the dirt like a lawn dart.

SIXTEEN

Present day
___

The boy sat in a porch chair with a feral kitten. Olea watched him as she swept.

He had a gangly handsomeness for his age and in spite of being covered in dirt. Thanks to her, he had a mop-head for a haircut and bangs that hid one eye or the other depending on his mood. Filth coated grime spread atop stains that patched his overalls and pullover, because he had farm animals for playmates and she was divested of proper detergent or a supermarket. He was as bright a child as she'd known and with a hot bath, proper barbering and a uniform he could be in a prep school, she thought, yet she could count the number of people he'd met outside of books on one hand. He was her David Copperfield, as graceful as the tomcats he played with, crusted in the day's scrapes and scabs, and lively as the runt he held.

"Why am I different?" He didn't look up.

This was the first she'd heard him mention it, but it must have been on his mind.

"I don't know. It's a mystery known only to God and Mother Nature." She kept at her sweeping as she spoke.

Nobel was at the barn corralling the goats while he mended their gate's torn leather hinges. He looked like an upright grasshopper, and she wondered what insect he saw her as, a wingless honeybee perhaps.

"Was my mother the same?"

"She was not."

Olea could see the family plot from where she stood. She'd introduced the boy to it as a treasured place where his mother slept, and they left bluets and coneflowers there regularly.

"What about my father?"

"I don't know that either but it's highly suspect."

"Which means no?"

"More or less."

The boy was old enough to learn the details of his life and they'd told him as much as they understood. He knew whose voice it was on the video recording but they'd withheld his viewing it. He stored no grudge against his mother, Olea told herself often, and wondered for whom she practiced the speech. Their affection was to keep the boy whole in spite of his privation. Just as the boy was closing chasms inside of them, Nobel once said.

"Are there other people in the world like me?"

"Are you wanting to be around other people, is that why you ask?"

The boy paled suddenly, as if his body recollected the time it had answered wrong.

"I didn't mean to threaten you. You know your papa only lives to protect you."

"And you."

"Are you afraid?"

"No."

"Is that the truth?"

"Is there a way for you to tell?"

He certainly had the germ of Nobel's intellect, she thought.

"It's not our way to declare our feelings, but you know my heart and your papa's belong to you."

"I do, but I don't know what that means."

"It means that he loves you as I do, and it's important for you to know that is the reason behind his rules. If you follow them, he won't take his axe to you again."

Olea chewed on her tongue and ultimately accepted that saying that without remorse wasn't possible.

The boy hugged the kitten fondly and stared at nothing in particular.

"I don't know how to believe something that's happened can't happen again."

Olea simply watched him. She lived in a straw house. There was no predicting when the wind would arrive, but it would come.

"There is a way to live without the past, child." Her voice weakened as she said this, like she'd fallen to her knees. She pulled a lace of roots from her broomcorn to hide herself.

"We can be safe here," she said finally.

"Can we?"

The boy was watching Nobel step past the garage. Its doors and windows were veneered in dust and hid the car abandoned inside. It was a mausoleum, Olea had once observed. Their farm tractor grew rust like coral beside it.

"Why are you and Papa the way you are?"

"The only answer to that question is to say because of the life we've had."

The boy stared at her like she was a parrot repeating

phrases.

"And the life of those who bore us, child, and bore them." Nobel was close enough. She could call him over.

"Does knowing that help you?"

"No," Olea confessed, startling herself. "I remember only a selection of events, curated by whom I don't know." If only Nobel would notice them and say something.

"Can memory be wrong?"

"It undoubtedly is, in some way." She leaned on her broom handle and let the boy study her, wrestling some leviathan in his mind. She could sense his heart beating faster, as his lungs emptied of air and his eyes darted left to right.

"Can you give me an example?"

"I can."

He wanted her response and she let him wait to calm them both.

"Boy?" She said at last. "You could recall when your papa took off your hand as proof that you are loved."

He didn't look convinced or contrary.

"Why else would a man so honorable do such a thing?"

The boy still reserved expression.

"You lost nothing and gained a faith in yourself, didn't you?"

As he kept his gaze on the kitten, Olea wished she could read his mind.

"Is that how you remember it, child?"

The boy didn't blink. He made no sound and moved only enough to stroke the kitten's fur sideways.

When he turned his eyes on her she felt a gust of nerves fill the cavity of her skull like helium. If her thoughts were light enough they might carry her away, she imagined.

"It is now," the boy said and set down the kitten with a

smile.

Olea noticed her toes try to grip the porch through her sandals. She was a little girl who'd fallen in the mud and hadn't been slapped.

"We share your feelings," was all she could say.

The boy just kept grinning and crawled onto the porch boards.

Watching him tease the kitten with a leaf Olea felt the urge to join, like when the boy used to hide in the vines and she'd grunt and snort searching for him like a boar and he'd laugh as if there wasn't foulness. They used to sit for dinner and Nobel would tell stories and stop suddenly and demand they choose what came next, tickling their ribs until they rejoined. That was how it was once, yet other moments had stolen rank. Perhaps the boy arranged his better.

"Tell me a story, Mamma."

She was his mother. What else did he have, or could she be?

"Okay," she said without thinking. "In the world you ask about, there is a beast."

The boy was hooked like a carp immediately, she saw. The kitten no longer ruled his attention.

"What does it do, the beast?"

"That is the sort of question a survivor would ask. It pretends to cure the shamed and worthless but gives them disease instead."

The boy became still.

"In the world away from here, people torment and kill the helpless to feed it," she hissed, playing her role in their melodrama.

"What people do that?"

"The sick."

"Who are the sick? How can you know them?"

"By their entitlement."

"I don't know what that means."

"It is a symptom, like the bite of a vampire, that makes a person unable to see themselves in reflection." The boy almost blenched, and she was thankful for how little he really knew of what was beyond their boundaries.

"How can you hide from them?"

"You cannot. At some point the sick and diseased will find you."

The boy was holding his breath.

"What are their names, child? The maladies that infest the world?"

"I don't know." He could only brave a whisper.

"They are greed and envy."

This made the boy stop. He twisted the leaf in his fingers until it was mulch. They kept a sofa outside until the winter made it useless and Olea sat on it.

The boy leaned forward and spoke in a hush as if they were sharing a ghost story over a campfire and had to keep the shadows from hearing.

"Who is the beast, momma?"

Olea let this sting her for a moment before she answered.

"It is the mind escaping,"

The boy's eyes widened in confusion. He inhaled slowly until his abdomen swelled to its limit. Then he took up Olea's broom and went about finishing the sweeping. Olea's shallow breath told her she wasn't as comfortable with the conclusion, and she watched him clear their porch of dust and detritus. She almost expected him to whistle like a dwarf.

"Now tell me the story of why you and Papa left everyone."

Olea felt a tremor that shook the chain on her neck and she

covered it with a hand.

They had left the world behind and as far as she could tell it had continued to degrade without them. They were better off here, even if their son had died too young without his mother and father, and so had his daughter, and so would her son.

Olea's throat compressed, like it was under a man's boot. She would do anything to save the boy and Nobel would die before he abandoned the child, but the world's bigotries were tics that couldn't be unscrewed without killing their host.

Her fingers clenched into fists. Nobel was right. She was fattening him, that's all. The boy would be devoured. A fire travelled through her spine and she hid her tears with a grin.

"After decades of strength, why does a bridge decide to collapse beneath a child?"

The boy stopped his sweeping to look at her and she used his face to warm hers.

"After centuries of stability, why does a landslide choose to fall on a family?"

The boy cocked his head. She felt hot metal poured onto her but he couldn't know.

"Which molecule of air can take credit for a hurricane? Do you know, child?"

The boy shook his head and she smiled as his bangs moved from left eye to right.

"Neither do I."

SEVENTEEN

Seventy years ago

Twenty-four hours before the log slipped from the truck it had been an old growth western red cedar.

Fourteen feet in diameter, it trampled Olea's father's skull like a chocolate covered cherry under a hoof. His dark hair tangled with the white of snow and red glaze of brain and bone. It wasn't a sight for an adult. Her mother's first instinct was not to cover Olea's eyes. Damning or not, Olea's mother did not consider her five-year-old child at all. Later if she caught Olea speaking of what she'd seen her mother would slap her and scold her for fibbing. Olea'd seen nothing because she'd been lovingly shielded.

In fact her mother dropped Olea's hand and fell to her knees onto the mix of coal and slush before the nearest live man. She clutched the gentleman's wool pant leg and ran a hand up to his belly beneath his coordinated jacket, tears smearing her makeup into the tarred eyes of a harlot about to be set on fire. Olea's father had pushed the two of them to the curb, and slipped on the oily sludge the fresh melt had drawn from the roadway. The truck had slowed for the passersby on the Bozeman city walk but its load chains were only partly set. An inebriated logger had rushed the clasp. A tree is a mighty thing compared to a man, only in its age, size and combustible power. Otherwise it is a lackey. Human misfortune was the writ cause that left Olea and her sister fatherless and their mother with no means or way.

Olea's widowed mother moved them to Olea's great aunt and uncle's, as her own parents were deceased. Olea and her sister were raised poorly but she did not starve and evaded the more severe physical abuses. Olea's great aunt and uncle followed the Bible like the pirate's map to salvation it was written to be. She credited their clarity of purpose for her pre-adolescent security.

When her mother found a new husband and gave Olea the choice of staying with her great aunt and uncle or coming with her and her younger sister, Olea chose to stay. Soon after her mother went to the mercantile to fill a grocery list and left Montana entirely with a traveller heading to California, and her sister returned.

Olea heard nothing from her until word came from the U.S. consulate in Mexico that her mother had been found dead with an arm removed. She'd held to enough allure to inveigle an oil baron of questionable charity to fit her with a diamond as big as a man's pinkie knuckle and manacle her wrist in hard candy-sized jewels. Her body had swollen from floating in saltwater. When she washed ashore a coconut machete was the most efficient way to relieve her of both treasures. There was no judicial will to determine a culprit or if the bruising on her face and torso had occurred prior to drowning. She'd fallen overboard was the official record.

As a youth Olea contemplated these details, and wondered if loss begets loss in a family tree.

EIGHTEEN

Fifty-eight years ago

Alcohol was subtle in a way other intoxicants failed to be. It slowly opened the curtain on the stage, that's how Olea described it.

She had been able to convince barkeeps and store clerks to serve her since the age of fifteen. By the time she was seventeen she knew every blues, juke and dance joint in western Missouri. Her great uncle had moved them to Kansas City to work the railroad stockyard until he retired.

"I'd like to go somewhere." Olea stood shivering on the frozen gravel.

"I'd like to take you there."

His hands were thick and the pants he wore were held up by a length of rope instead of a belt but the pea jacket he wore was new and the turned-up collar framed his puffed head like a hedgehog girdled in a drainpipe.

"I'm not interested in going just anywhere."

"I promise to make it interesting." His chest was a barrel

wrapped in a canvas vest and he had to duck to step through the doorway.

"Don't go making guarantees. We just met."

Something magical happened to Olea when she drank the clear liquors. She could laugh, sing, howl and leave a man searching for his prairie oysters. The first time she was touched as a woman, she was eleven and taller than the other girls but not mistakable for a menstruating virgin. The neighbor lived with his infirm mother and was appreciated for his sinewy arms and a voice that wasn't country ragged. He poured Olea a gin, soda and sugar water. She asked him what he thought her father would think of their communion, and he said her father would not understand their bond. She told him that he was right, because her father understood nothing but the worms that burrowed through his brain. She didn't resist. His kiss had a formaldehyde wetness and he smelled of mothballs. Then he let her be. There was no separating romance and danger, she thought, and growing wouldn't change that.

"My truck is just around the corner." His voice had a nasal quality like a pinched balloon releasing air.

"I'll take a taste from that bottle to keep me warm."

"By all means, wet your whistle." He handed her the bottle caped in yesterday's paper. "Your old man works the yards in Cow Town."

"He's my great uncle."

"I'd bet a week's wage your bed sheets smell like manure."

Olea uncapped the bottle and tossed the tin lid into the snow.

"You're not the first fellow to think vulgarity would subdue a woman's need to be wooed." Olea took a long pull, filling her cheeks before she swallowed.

Her favorite part was when they peeled off her clothing until no onion layer remained, just desolation. The winter months were wildest. The colder the weather, the bigger the onion. The stubbier a man's fingers, the more calloused, the more numbed by icy air, the more he struggled with her feminine zippers, clasps and buttons. Even the lace thin elastic of her undergarments often proved harder for a man to pinch than a strand of hair on a bar of soap. She chose the ones who would take their time. Most had no choice. Mesmerized by the forthcoming softness of her skin, clear and pale, they slowed in snorting awkwardness, spluttering huffs of air to control their unfulfilled anticipation as a pea sized snap slipped from their fingertips like a greased ball bearing.

Once she was fully birthed, she enjoyed the air and scent of sweat and petrol that came off with the men's mildewed wool and cotton shells. The first moment, when their bristled skin and the warm press of their muscled fat pinned her, like a plucked flower slipped between the pages of a book and forgotten, she felt like a defect was about to be repaired. The rest was the ugly grunting mechanics of completing the act without becoming pregnant. A crescendo of squelching followed by a tumultuous apogee of moose calls, and every man she invited in to remove her filth left a splash of sewage instead. Their deposits flushed her emptiness with butcher's waste, stuffing her like a sow's stomach, stretching a membrane inside of her that would never burst.

We're born full vessels and before we can remember, our guardians empty us to catch their runoff like bedpans. Their parasite hatches in our void and grows as us, and who we are becomes the riddle we never solve. This secret ruled the world. You sought what was taken from you, and you were what filled its place.

"There's someone already in your truck." They were otherwise alone in a desert of frozen ink.

"That's a friend of mine." The figure in the cab shifted and flipped on the cab's dome light, revealing a second.

"Unless that friend has a Siamese twin, I'd say you're being humble." Olea could see the two figure's mouths steam inside the cab, exhaling in rhythm like the nostrils of a giant snout.

"They'll make room for you to ride their lap."

"I'd prefer to go back." Olea said, and was open to both interpretations. The man grabbed her shoulder tightly with his brawny mitt. It was not to keep her warm.

"If you met us each, one day after the other, or served us together at once, what difference would it be to you?"

Olea had loosely held to the dream that one of the port and rail encrusted roadmen, travellers or county servant eggs she brooded regularly would one day hatch a prince.

She'd been given the emperor's new clothes as a chemise cagoule and paved her way with good intentions, she liked to tell bartenders, but she hadn't seen the bottom coming.

"You aren't the company I'd hoped to have when I turned up my toes."

The man spun her and slapped her across the mouth. His hand had the sandpaper softness of a brick, she noticed.

"Do not play superior to me, nor what's coming to you."

Olea could feel the blood cooling on her lip and pooling under her tongue. There was a time she would've fought back in spite of the beating it unleashed, but hadn't she taken the road for this very reason? She hoped it would suit God to introduce himself before the defiling.

"I'd like you to end this now. I'd rather warm up the beetles and let you and your friends continue to prosper in the cold."

The man balled his fingers into a club and brought it back. She braced for the blow and a white light illumed and cast their shadows fleeing backward, parallel to infinity.

Was this more devils arriving late to the party, or her end of the tunnel? Olea wondered, shading her eyes from the headlights.

Her abductor halved the liquor bottle on the tarmac and pulled her closer.

"Get yourself lost! This is a private matter!"

His shouting roused his partners from the truck. Both threw black tails that disappeared in the woods alongside hers.

Olea envisioned herself a spirit watching her body eaten, and a red flash cut the fog, revolving above the white beams, coloring the haze like a lighthouse with blood on its lens.

"As Jackson County Police, I am appointed to protect its persons with deadly force."

The slide chambering of a Browning 12-gauge echoed against the quiet, and Olea felt her misfortune recede like an eel into its hole.

.

NINETEEN

Three years ago

Nobel couldn't tell if he was bleeding internally.

"Come out slowly or you won't come out at all."

"We are both injured in this plane, my friend, I think you know." Came the voice of the pilot.

What a threesome they made.

Nobel was in no condition to carry one man, let alone two while leaking to death. He could jury-rig a sled with saplings lashed together and use his stallion as a sleigh dog, but that would mean limping back to the homestead. He should just shoot them both. He'd let the wheat and kudzu grow over, and tell anyone looking for the plane he knew nothing of it. He was old, deaf and almost sightless, and had missed the crash for all they knew. Let their compadres or pursuers find it on their own, if they had his coordinates. Of course he knew the truth was if anyone did come looking, they would likely kill him, Olea and the boy, but torture them first to ensure no one else knew about what had fallen at the foot of their rainbow.

As a judge he'd heard the story of a Honduran mercenary who'd forced a man from Arkansas to mutilate his own wife to save their child from being boiled alive, only to catch the man in a lie and deflower his daughter on his lap before massacring them all.

Nobel pulled the rifle's bolt to his cheek. This was a fine kettle of fish.

"We cannot exit on our own, my friend."

"Why?" The boy said, standing alone between Nobel and the plane.

Olea was on their remaining mare with the scattergun they used to buckshot grouse on her knee. She was behind Nobel and not in sight of the plane yet, and saw him looking at her. His position behind his dead nag would paint the picture.

The boy must have come on his own, or they'd rode in double and he was meant to keep his distance while she made her approach. He would have taken the length through the corn alone. Nobel held up a hand, keeping Olea back. The boy stood at the ordnance the men had tossed from the wreck. Nobel could see it all, two bleeding killers staring at a six-year-old alone in a field of green grain beside a submachine gun and semi-automatic pistol. If they had a third weapon, the boy could be gunned down before he or Olea could snatch him.

"Come to me, boy" Nobel shouted.

The boy just stared at him and then bent and picked up the gold-plated firearm.

"Leave it and come this way."

"Ven aqui, m'ijo." The copilot countered. "Venga. Niño. Boy. We need help. Por favor. Please."

The boy looked at the plane.

The men only needed the boy to sway him and Olea to do their bidding.

Nobel stood up and felt the bee sting at his hip.

"Boy. Wait there. I'm coming to you."

Nobel saw the pilot shift as the copilot continued his outcry.

"Come this way. Hurry, child. Come to me, niño. We need your help."

Nobel shouldered his rifle and fired. The bullet struck the control panel and the echoing crack shut everyone up.

The copilot jerked in his seat, clanging his cage walls to no avail and the pilot spoke.

"I have a son of my own. We do not need anyone to be hurt."

He held rank, Nobel thought, and took the gun from the boy and tossed it and the other toward Olea, his eyes never leaving the cockpit.

"Stay here, boy." Nobel said, and approached the inverted fuselage.

It took every jot of strength he had to gimp the distance and keep his barrel trained.

Both men stared at him from within the shadowed cabin, two saucer-eyed bats woken from sleep.

When the beak of the plane struck, the instrument panel had snapped on their legs like a mousetrap.

Their cargo had fallen to the roof. It was in wooden boxes long enough a single man couldn't carry them. Munitions maybe, or explosives. That would explain the fervor. He should have thought of that, before he went firing random shots.

The tumbling had freed one of the box's lids and he pushed it aside. It was impossible to get a good look and still keep his 30-30 trained on the two men.

They scrutinized him like they had poison tongues, they'd sling the second he dropped his guard.

"What's in the boxes?" Neither answered. "If it's rattle snakes or land mines and I survive I'll shoot the nose from your face. The muzzle flash will probably blind you, so be comforted you won't have to look at yourselves."

Both men remained silent.

Nobel readied his gun and the pilot spoke again.

"Go ahead. Find out. Then please help us."

Could it be possible they didn't know? Nobel's wound seemed stable but he had his own diminishing hourglass. He leaned in and brushed aside a handful of packing straw.

"Papa."

"Stay back now."

The boy had split the distance separating them. Nobel could see Olea closing, on foot behind him, carrying the shotgun in the hook of her arm. She'd unsaddled and tied her horse to one of the plane wings.

"Who'd you tell you were bellying up here?"

Nobel got no response, so he shoved his rifle nose into the copilot's ear hard enough to prune a piece off.

The man hollered for a few seconds and twisted his head to glare at Nobel but said nothing.

"Who knows you touched down? Quién sabe?" Nobel repeated.

"The answer to that is very valuable to you, is it?"

The pilot seemed to be daring Nobel to test the grit of his ear.

"What's in the plane with them?" Olea shouted.

She had the boy behind her now, with a hand on his head, the MP7 over her shoulder and the gilded .45 tucked into her belt. It was a sight to see, Olea heavily armed in a house dress and muddy boots and the boy in a shirt stitched from a curtain and a hat darned from an old sweater sleeve.

"I'm not sure I want to know," he said, but not loud enough she was guaranteed to hear.

He was holding to the possibility of a way out for everyone. Would they or their people really have a reason to kill him if he knew nothing of their doings? He knew them as men who'd fired on him because they'd been rattled like a marble in a tin and he was carrying a rifle. That alone could be proven.

"What's the road out for us all?"

The pilot studied Nobel, measuring his fiber most likely.

Blood dripped off the men at arrhythmic intervals, like dew off a stalactite pooling on the upholstered ceiling. It was almost comical, the two of them attempting to terrorize him while strung upside down.

Nobel knew better than to laugh, but was losing patience.

"A lever, some rope, and my surviving cob mare and I can shuck you like a quahog."

The pilot was starting to look pale in spite of his dark complexion. The white in one eye had steeped red and a gash percolated in his thigh, dribbling coagulant like candle wax down his trunk, where it gathered in a putrid marsh in his black beard. He hid his left hand, which tremored of its own will, and his nostrils spread with each breath as his lungs strained to expand. He motioned to his cheek. A chip of bone had been torn off with a cap of skin.

"You shot me."

"You killed my horse."

"Where's your granada?"

"I lied about possessing it. That doesn't make us even."

The pilot's eyes found the wet stain on Nobel's side.

"You were policia?" In spite of his grotesque appearance the pilot had an affable quality. "So was I."

"That's hard to envision," Nobel said, and realized it had

been too long since he'd spoken to another man.

The pilot was in his late forties, at least a decade older than the copilot.

"Look into the box, amigo. Then we can discuss our options."

"What's he saying to you?" Olea couldn't risk leaving the boy to die or survive as a wild child without them, so she kept her distance.

"He wants me to investigate their cargo before we agree on our collusion."

Sometimes you can only think so many moves ahead, he thought, and put his hand beneath the filling straw and pulled out a black plastic bag. It was heavy with something shaped like a broken melon. Nobel spun it. The bag had torn during the box's flip-flop, and a cloudy eyeball gaped out at him from its orbit in a chimp's head.

The rest of the swelling ape was bagged and packed beneath, dressed in a Liga MX Club América jersey and denim shorts. During shipment the pullover had rolled up over the torso and exposed a pink brassiere. This detail was especially disturbing. The headless chimpanzee had a zip-locked baggie in its gorgon fingers. The sandwich bag contained a detached phallus, wreathed midway in a molar-sized engagement setting, likely positioned with two pairs of pliers given the contusions. It brought to mind a misfired cattle bander. Human or simian, he couldn't tell. Either was quite a message.

Nobel hadn't the stomach for the other crates, and postponed the exploration.

TWENTY

The second plane wing was sheared in thirds and the smallest segment fit both men supine.

They were not further armed.

Nobel had uncorked them from their snare and fastened a makeshift bobsleigh as planned. He rode atop Olea's cob, holding the boy in his lap and towing the sickly pair, while Olea walked them all home.

The copilot's shinbones had both been snapped, the right protruded like a tree branch dangling shavings of dermis like a fall molt of reddened leaves. Nobel did his best to set both, and he moaned in and out of unconsciousness. Olea had tied off the pilot's bleeding gouge and other than the luster of dehydration he looked improved.

Nobel would clean and patch his own bullet hole and return to the plane in the morning to give it a thorough comb. That was the best he could do.

He retrieved a set of cuffs from a box of leftover patrolman ephemera that he'd saved. He knew his fortitude wouldn't top theirs for long, and clamped the pilot's wrist to one of the copilot's ankles. Given the segundo's condition, this would do for the night. Even if the pilot chose to strangle his partner, the noise of it and dragging the dead man's weight or trying to remove the foot would wake the house in time for Nobel to put a muzzle to his head. He had found no identification or mobile device on either. Perhaps their personals had catapulted in the set down. He'd look tomorrow.

Olea helped Nobel bathe and gave the clotted holes on his side clean dressing. She didn't ask many questions, knowing he had barely the energy to nod his head. At least for the moment they were safe.

TWENTY-ONE

Nobel woke in the middle of the night to whispering.

The house was dark except for the light of the fires. He eased himself out of bed, unable to remember how he'd gotten there.

The boy was sitting cross-legged on the floor, a gamin just out of harm's range like he'd seen the cats do to Bill when he was chained to a tree. The copilot slept fitfully and the pilot sat up facing the child.

"Why is your skin dark?"

"Because of my mother and father." The pilot slid his palm out onto the lake of floor before him to test his reach.

"Did they do something to you?"

"No. They just fed me. Their skin was the same."

The boy looked at the pilot like he was Ali Baba himself.

"Is there a vehicle, an auto here?" The pilot shifted.

"Yes."

"Does it function?"

"It's in the garage."

"You could show me?" He smiled at the boy like a father, his black beard knotted with peanuts of congealed blood.

"Will you be here long?"

"I do not expect so."

The boy stared at the sleeping copilot whose breath burbled like a radiator filling with steam.

"Perhaps I will return with my son."

The boy stuck his finger through a hole in his pajamas and pushed the nail edge into his skin.

"Your son is not like me."

"Why do you say this?"

"You will think so too."

The pilot nipped his dry lips together, observing the boy, and the floorboards interrupted him as Nobel stepped toward them both.

"Come to bed with us, boy."

"We're just talking." The boy grinned up at Nobel.

"I'm aware. This hour's for sleeping."

"I want to sit with the visitors."

"You can do so tomorrow."

"They're the first to be let inside. I'm afraid they'll be gone."

After six years with only Olea and him as companions, he realized a fencepost with a hat on it could charm the boy. The irony was, he'd given these two the honor.

"I say they'll sit for your visit in the morning, so you can believe it. Yes?"

"Yes, Papa." The boy stood and walked backward into the bedchamber.

The pilot regarded Nobel from below.

"If you've internal injuries, you'll need more than that

patch-job."

"I could say the same. No, Capitán? You hold my life in your hand, so you think. This is what you mean to say."

Nobel had done hundreds of interrogations and no matter the crime, even the hint of a menace in a man sent a charge through him. The room brightened for a moment, but he didn't show it.

"You may learn how age diminishes a man's charity. You may not."

Nobel had nothing more to say, yet stood his ground and the pilot lowered his eyes. This wasn't his first negotiation for a human life. He knew when to lie down.

There was an old thousand pound plow half-buried beside the back steps. Nobel took a three-quarter-inch logger's chain he'd forfeited to rust, looped it through the digger's iron brace beam and cross-shaft, wound it around the handcuff links and bolted the ends with a penitentiary lock his father had passed on to him.

Neither of them could walk but he would support his fate with vigilance.

He then took a dented copper boiler from under the porch that Bill had used as a water dish and kicked it across the home's fir boards. It bumpered between the two men.

The pilot's expression said he understood. It would be their latrine.

TWENTY-TWO

Nobel rode Olea's mare with the first glow to the wreck.

He spooked the crows and buzzards with his arrival.

In her stillness, his dead horse seemed to lean earthward with her shoulder, trying to hasten her natural interment and cheat the sorrow of her state.

Coyotes drawn by the scent of blood and muscle had tossed the insides of the plane. He kicked himself for not foreseeing this.

From where he stood he could see they'd worked the bloat of his mare and exposed her ribs like a ship run aground. The gourmands had pealed the skin around her skull like a hard-boiled egg, and her lips and lids were gnawed off like cracklings. They'd left her gaping at him with a terrified smile, her mane fouled with bird droppings and coon retch, the remains of her eye sockets pecked out, their spill and her tongue fragments already collecting worms on the wet scrub. It wasn't a fitting burial. Nobel added the image to the pyre growing beneath their visitors.

It took him better than four hours, but he searched every inch of the plane and its debris and the fifty yards of seedling wheat, brome and indiangrass around it. He even pulled apart the inhumed engine.

The chimp had been torn to pieces, her hirsute shreds and garment bits spread about haphazard in their tug-of-wars. He imagined the poor thing, blind without her head, stepping on a landmine, as he combed through the gamy chunks he found like Easter eggs.

The sandwich bag and its contents were gone. So was the fickle migration of the species, a wanderer in some implausible location might find the giant engagement stone one day in a pile of coyote scat and pizzle remains, and believe themselves selected by God.

He located no identification, registry plates or discriminating items. They'd pitched anything that could tell their story or link them to the aircraft, either before takeoff or once falling was a certainty, even their keys. In all, he'd collected a pillbox, a magazine of alloy-plated rounds, the cellophane from a pack of cigarettes, a hawkbill knife, and two disposable cell phones. One was destroyed. The other stored a testimony of photos, but otherwise didn't function because of their remoteness. They had no reason to ditch a satellite phone in their dive. It would've been needed, particularly if he hadn't arrived.

He couldn't be sure but Nobel felt the pendulum of luck swinging his direction.

He'd left the sealed cargo boxes until last.

Their fasteners had held off the scavengers. He pulled each from the hull with a length of cordage and his horse.

They lay askew on the trampled crop, midget coffins made of crate wood.

Each a jack-in-the-box with a monster inside, Nobel thought, and was paused by memory.

The connect-the-dots puzzle he had drawn from child to pensioner made a picture only a greater power could decipher. The image of himself at the boy's age was as foreign as a Martian.

He removed the nails from each box lid with a pry bar and recalled that in France they called the winding toy a boxed devil.

He thought he heard the breeze whistle *Pop Goes The Weasel* through the bluestem, and laughed at his jitters. Then the innards of a crate made a thud.

He froze and stared at all three, counting breaths to thirty. No other sound came. The shifting of their positions or a field rat had done it, he told himself and flung the covers from each, like a street performer opening cobra baskets.

Their cargo was similarly packaged, in black bags.

To preserve the integrity of the goods and contain odor, presumably, and to prolong the torment of surprise. A layer of black tissue, found within a lunatic's wrapped present.

In one was a decapitated man who'd been bent in half for bagging, and packed with a woman's head. A circle of fabric was cut from the crotch of the man's trousers and underwear like a spotlight on an empty stage. The missing pecker had been human. The second contained a woman's headless corpse similarly crimped, and the man's removed skull. His mouth was filled with excrement. In all his years, he'd never seen anything like it. From the nature and state of the wounds, Nobel loosely deduced the chain of events and the fellow came out the loser.

In the final box was two million in Canadian currency, guarded by ninety-three teddy bears of different shapes and colors.

He approximated the payout by flipping a dozen straps and generalizing by volume, but counted out the stuffed animals.

It would take forensics or a family member to identify the couple, but given their figures and attire, Nobel guessed they were approaching middle age, well-heeled and by the man's tattoos, not from this country. Their rigor mortis had slacked. It had been over a day since they'd been killed together, but not much more. Reconstructed they made a family of three. Someone had clearly felt scorned by one or all, although it was hard to surmise how a circus primate could engender such contempt.

The unidentified party remained the individual or organization meant to receive the trio. As punishment and warning, or proof that a damaged heart or reputation had been refunded. The tableau could also simply complete the torture of someone whose destiny was to lose everything. Regardless, *You can run but you can't hide* was the apparent caption.

There was a rudimentary drawing on a torn sheet of paper at the bottom of the third box. It was meant to be assembly instructions, and looked like it was done by a halfwit. The geld man with the woman's head, the chimp wearing the man's bell tower and gripping his bagged sausage like a clutch, and the woman's belfry topped with a chimp mascaron. This was the proposed diorama, demented but undoubtedly memorable.

It was impossible to concoct the exact scenario. A jealous husband or lover, a spurned father or associate, vengeance for an equal or lesser deed, or a disagreement between warring clans. None of which fully explained the reduced ape and her stuffed bedmates.

At what point did human communication require such a vernacular to convey a point of view, Nobel wondered on the ride back to the homestead, with the Canadian fortune in tow.

All three victims wore clothing they weren't killed in, which meant someone redressed a headless primate as a teenage girl. It wasn't a mental picture he'd ever expected to have, and he had to accept that he might never know why so many teddy bears had to witness such a grisly performance.

There was no way to determine if the men he had locked up were responsible for just the delivery, or the executions as well. The good news was, unless it had been inserted into one of the cadavers or ingested, there was no tracking device.

Nobel could see the chimney smoke rise like steam from his rooftop, and imagined its view of his homecoming.

He was no blood and thunder hero. He wore a chaparral for hair and a dry lakebed for a face. His muscles were cracked elastic nailed to creaking ship timbers and his hinges pulsated as he flapped in time with the horse's step. Yet he sat as straight as a young man.

What have I invited inside? He asked Olea's horse.

The two men were the first people the boy had seen up close. They'd seen him as well. The quickness of it and the child's curiosity had limited Nobel's options. But the truth was, his haste had opened a can of worms and he'd moved them into it.

He'd become a deputy to fight exactly this infection, a prosecutor to contain it, and a judge to find an antidote. But still depravity replicated, like plague in the crevices of pork.

The first pill you swallowed was only a pittance of justice existed. Inertia gobbled up the choicest meat and he parceled what fell from the table, he used to say.

By now, however, he'd stepped back enough to see the Rube Goldberg machine in its entirety, and concluded where the law was concerned the strings of the sow's ear were tied and untied by interests he simply didn't understand.

He'd spent his career chasing his tail, and retired with it between his legs.

The question remained, if this was the culmination of his lifetime of distributing justice, what illness possessed him that he continued to sacrifice for it?

TWENTY-THREE

Fifty-eight years ago

The squad car sat alone in the choppy sea of bituminous pitch and snow.

He could smell the turpentine hint of potato liquor beneath her flower scent beside him. She clasped herself for warmth so tightly it looked like she'd purchased her jacket from a mental ward's rummage sale. He almost said so, but decided she hadn't known him long enough to get his humor. Instead he started the engine and cranked up the heater.

She rocked slowly with her knees hugging, tilted together away from him, pinching the seat between her heels and thighs. He could tell she was exercising her toes for circulation, or to see if they were still there. Her big ones tightly huddled each other naked beneath her wet shoe leather, he imagined, and felt ashamed for invading her privacy.

"It's kind of you to take me in." The red eyes of the three men's taillights dissolved into the haze. "Sending them home, instead of locking them up, was also brotherly."

She was still catching her air, and worried she sounded flip.

"I'm familiar with their habits. It won't take long, and they'll know my jail better than their homes."

Nobel studied the dashboard.

"Your jail?" She leaned over and read his name off the vehicle registry. "You are an ambitious lawman, *Deputy Nobel.*"

He sensed her lips bend up, but didn't confirm it.

"I thin wolves from the herd, at the pleasure of the county. If that's your word for it, I'll give it to you."

"Then I've endured on the chivalry of a cowboy."

"Who said anything about cows?"

Caught off guard, Olea hiccupped a hee-haw of laughter.

Unable to stop himself, Nobel giggled through his clenched lips as well.

The cab was getting milder. They could no longer see their breath, but she kept a tight hold of herself still, like she was comforting a sufferer.

"I wish you'd hauled them in."

"Under what charge?"

"Conspiracy to pirate a lady's warmth and dignity. Clearly."

She watched Nobel drill on a tooth with his tongue like he wanted it removed.

"They weren't so drunk, they won't try to repair their pride on another dummy. A lady alone, who's less looked after." She tried to add a grin. "I'll walk home with hoarfrost for clothes, if it will save her."

He felt her look at him sideways.

"That thought you're chewing on just outlived a mayfly." She winked to hide her unease.

"I am just a deputy. One of those fellows has relations more powerful than our two families put together going back to the cavemen. I lock them up on no charge tonight, when I catch them breaking the law, an attorney in a suit that would cost me a year's salary will call it escalating harassment by a peace officer." His demeanor said it had happened before. "If I arrest them now, the county will try your character in their stead."

Olea's chin convulsed forward and back.

"Then you've spared me from more than one ruining." Her voice peeped, like she was in a cat's mouth.

She was a schoolgirl caught bathing, with soap in her eye. There was no comfort he could give, being a man.

"Thank goodness for the cold or you'd see my cheeks going rosy, deputy."

Nobel watched her take in air until she'd filled her bosom, which drew attention to her clutched arms and she released them, freeing a drowned soul to sink into the murk.

They sat in silence, until the temperature demanded he dial down the fan.

"Was your father a policeman?"

He didn't hear her question, but she knew the answer.

"Those three will commit acts that a judge will see fit for prison. When they do, I'll bunk them with menfolk who will know them in a way that they'll understand as justice. That's a promise I'll carry like Atlas."

He couldn't look at her, she noticed.

"You'll catch them during an assault on private property or the state flag maybe? While they're violating something of value, like a mailbox or a lawn ornament for example?"

She hoped to embarrass him but could see he was giving it consideration, and suddenly feared he'd be offended and hand her back to the glacier of black paint outside.

"The law favors a man, because the bulwarks of privilege are themselves," he said at last. "I have faith that the county will correct this in our lifetime."

"You'd better pray for a quick humbling of all mankind then, deputy," she said and guffawed with a snort so uncensored she covered her mouth with both hands to hide her face.

Her eyes widened, and Nobel almost laughed as she retreated against the passenger door.

Her first-day-of-school smile implied two things. Her certainty of the failures of men, and that she wouldn't outlive the season much less the era.

"Have you already given up so thoroughly?" It was unexpected candor.

Olea felt insulted. She uncurled her posture, furious with herself for showing too much and at him for seeing it.

"How about a gold star on your uniform for your choice detectiving, Deputy Nobel?" Her voice was sober. "Or is life in the catbird seat reward enough?"

Nobel returned to reading his speedometer.

He was so earnest. It was embarrassing.

The vibrating engine block purred for them both, until they'd been stripped like kittens licked after birth.

"At least you're safe now," Nobel finally said, and Olea felt her surface go in a landslide and found herself staring at the pine needles jellied in mud on the floor mat.

"I didn't mean to imply that later you won't be."

Her hands crawled off her lap and burrowed under her hips.

"I apologize," he said and saw her pupils move to his like he'd reeled them in.

She looked like she'd been cloistered under a bed and someone had overturned it.

"Don't apologize."

Nobel stared at her like he was behind two-way glass, aware

that her effect was exposing on his face. The moment lasted long enough that when he spoke his voice was different.

"I don't fear the evil of men."

"I can see that."

She knew there was a second part he was leaving out, and said it for him.

"But you're terrified of the good of a woman."

His jaw rippled and he didn't speak.

His head rocked forward and back, and he put the squad car in gear and drove from the lot.

TWENTY-FOUR

Three years ago

The chair made a coital groan with the floor as Nobel drug it to the mudroom door and sat before the two men.

"I don't believe anyone knows you're here."

They were on their backs at the acme of their chain's length.

"Someone far away funded your trip, I think."

The copilot's breath was fleshy. He had gone feverish and twitched involuntarily.

"Neither of you have the teeth of a wealthy man."

The pilot's leg had swollen around its bandage, and neither man appeared amused by Nobel's inserting of puzzle pieces.

"I presume you chose a proven smuggling route up and got off course on return." Nobel set down their working and destroyed cell phones on the floor between his feet.

The copilot eyeballed each like a child presented a vase he'd broken.

"You sent photographs before you departed." Nobel said

nothing more.

"We are good men. Es verdad lo que digo." The copilot looked like a hound that had given over to mange.

"Your engine failure was an act of God. The rest was an act of character." Nobel kept his eyes on the pilot.

The copilot's lips parted again to speak and the pilot took their chain in his free hand and gave the cuff around his partner's ankle a casual tug. The shock of pain caused the copilot to bite his tongue like he'd had a seizure and he spit a gob of bloody phlegm onto the floorboards.

"You have not notified your authorities." The pilot looked at Nobel as if they shared kin.

"I am my own authority."

Olea could be heard shuffling behind Nobel, tending to the stove, while the boy spied from the front porch. The two men looked like animate road kill but Nobel had to accept there was no hope either would expire on their own without assistance.

"What you're saying is that we have nothing to bargain with, not even your human kindness." The pilot had a beggar's tact but wasn't used to playing the weaker hand.

Nobel wondered if either man had read his hesitation to involve others or saw his reluctance to graduate from judge and jury. It didn't matter, Nobel concluded. His quarrel wasn't with another man ultimately.

"When you don't arrive your employer, or whomever is waiting for you, will assume you perished on your way."

"An assumption you hope to make true."

"Hope left the party when you two dropped in."

The pilot was a practiced snake. They were guilty, but he hadn't shown a tell of arrogance or whit of capitulation. He wanted Nobel to turn them in. Or was he bluffing, or had Nobel revealed more than he knew and the pilot had realized there was more at stake than just their lives? He'd definitely used the word *hope* with intimation.

Throughout his years as a lawman Nobel had consciously denied his imagination the role of the hangman, because he wasn't willing to risk what might follow. Now he was a scarecrow delaying the blackbirds from his fields with parley.

They could all see Olea from their spot, and the men's eyes ignited with fire each time she opened the potbelly's door and threw in a ten-thousand-dollar bundle of Canadian banknotes.

The pilot's tongue darted out and made a futile attempt to wet his lips and he and the copilot looked up at Nobel in unison like two heads of a hydra.

Nobel knew if somehow they did succeed in finding a way out of this, they would sure as the tide return, even if the earth itself buckled up in all its powerfulness to stop them.

Nobel did not want to but suddenly saw himself, Olea and the boy splayed out on the grit, their domes and extremities exchanged according to some dimwit's drawing on a napkin.

TWENTY-FIVE

Fifty-eight years ago

The tenement Olea's great Aunt and Uncle kept was crumbling and full of cow yard workers and their families, and the people who survived because of them.

Olea took a corner of piecrust and closed the piece up. At this hour almost all of the lights were out. She set the small white box on the sedan's dash shelf and caught sight of her door handle. It was an ejector lever, she envisioned, and felt childish.

"That's yours to take with you."

"You keep it. I've had my share."

He didn't fully hear her. The sheriff markings on his cruiser were drawing rubbernecks from the passing topers, as they shambled home. She watched him survey her trash-strewn street and its paupers like he was protecting an empire.

"You are a man of serious contemplation, Deputy Nobel."

Caught off guard, he tucked his chin once, like a stallion backed up.

"You can call me Mason."

"I'll call you Nobel, if it's alright?"

"Most people do."

"I like the way that sounds."

She reserved her eyes as she said this so not to appear too flirty. He was only a few years her senior but he seemed so grownup.

Nobel had a view of Olea's building and watched a fellow ogle her from against the brick like she was his private figurine. The way the man leaned with his eyes lowered, Nobel wanted to cuff his snout with his baton. He reached for it, and comprehended what was happening within him.

Another stray lad passed and gawped at Olea openly. She was just out of high school, and he looked at her as if she was his peach to pick. Was this the world of an appealing young woman?

Nobel steamed air from his nose, like a horse thrashing the gate. Olea noticed his glowering.

"Nobel?"

She impulsively touched his hand to calm his spinning top, and he woke like a boy from a spell but didn't say a word.

"I'm glad the county sees me unfit to protect."

"The county is my employer." She'd meant that he saw her differently, he understood after he'd spoken. "If I'm fit for a judge's robe one day, I promise to tend the scales better."

"You're just full of promises. Do junior deputies often use a magistrate's tailor?"

"They do. After law school and a significant amount of prosecutorial experience."

He said this so humorlessly, she couldn't keep her face from chuckling. This surprised him enough that he went flush.

"Do you keep promises as well as Minos did to Poseidon?"

"Better than."

"I hope so."

"You've turned a page." He said, and tossed his eyes, admitting he was beyond his depth.

"I've read a book or two. Did you know they let the fairer sex into libraries now?" Olea winked reflexively and bit the puff of her lip. "Or did you mean in the other sense?"

He grinned for his answer, unable to speak. A lightness was replacing the tension in his chest. He'd dropped a weight he hadn't known he was carrying. It was dizzying and he elevated in his seat. She'd intoxicated him, he thought, as he talked out of turn.

"There are things that can take place between a man and a woman that words will never do justice."

"Are we having one of those things?"

"I believe we are."

"Do these things last between a man and a woman?"

"This time they do."

Nobel's certainty had him running ahead without her, he worried. He held the air in his lungs to keep quiet but didn't take his eyes from her.

Olea wrung her hands and scooted herself further from her exit. They were two groundhogs avoiding their shadow, she told herself, that was it.

"What's got you scared?"

"Besides that this is going to end too soon?"

If he would just look away, she could put her armor back on.

"I know there's something that's got a hook in you."

Olea went stiff. If he touched her, she would shatter. He knew it and didn't move a muscle.

"There are no monsters I can't safeguard you from."

It should've sounded like boasting, but he'd meant it.

"Another promise?" She jabbed to give him space, but found herself confessing before he could take it. "I will say the hallway to my uncle's door is long."

"I don't follow. Please. One more time, for the simple."

"Imagine a cat saved from her spot up a tree, and brought to the pound." She was trying to be witty, but her face told him the truth without her consent.

His hands went heavy.

"I feel very lucky, Nobel, but I don't feel fortunate."

Terror in a man had no affect on Nobel, he'd actually grown to enjoy it, but seeing it in Olea pulled a trigger in him that couldn't be undone. His pulse started to thump faster and his neck and face got hot.

"There's a church that has beds for those without them."

"Okay," she said, knowing she wouldn't survive the night.

"I'll stay there," he finished. "You'll have my home."

Olea watched him stare into the theater lit by his headlights. She grasped the ways of men like a woman three times her age, and gripped her door handle.

"That's a kind offer, deputy, but regardless of my feelings, you've no reason to trust in me, and a man without reason is a dangerous thing."

"Don't make me for a hothead, Olea, but without reason I'd be piling bodies on that sidewalk quicker than this sentence was finished."

He looked at her in a way she'd never experienced. His body was steady and his breath was anchored. He wasn't outraged, she realized. He was devoted.

She studied him like he was a dinosaur or a dodo bird. He was an apparition only she could see, and her hand fell from the latch.

TWENTY-SIX

Present Day

The barrow hit every rock and root that stuck its frozen back out of the game trail, like he was following a pod of miniature whales trapped in an arctic freeze.

He carted a hemp sack he'd filled with Ella's valise and all its original contents, the pink-haired doll and video camera and cassette, as well as everything they'd ever made for the boy or that he'd marked. His clothes, drawings and toys, and the tools Nobel had fashioned for his size. Other than the psychological cave paintings he'd scratched on their insides, only the boy's body and the clothes on it proved he existed.

"Boy, you're not a man but I'm at the end of what I can fathom." He said between efforts. "It's possible because of your age you're a better receiver for higher message."

"What higher message?"

"Whatever speaks to you without language, in your muscles."

"Speaks how then?"

"What you know without a word or image pinned to it is what I mean."

"You want me to help you with what can't be put in words?"

Nobel plodded the ceramic ground like an ox in mud and spoke just as well.

"Do you feel that you belong in this world?"

"What do you mean belong?"

"What's your gut reaction?"

The boy bent to pick up a rock and threw it.

"My gut says there's something you want to hear said."

"If there was ever a doubt we're related you're proving it once and for all."

> The boy looked at him like he was wearing clown makeup.

"What does it feel like to belong?"

"It feels like a need to be, and to contribute to the growing fungus of humankind."

"You're just being funny."

"Boy, you're going to have to leap. Be spoken through, like a howl."

Nobel felt his mania hawking at him and slowed his pace. A lamp of witches' butter shown up at him through the grey proving life persevered beneath the glaze.

The boy hid his hands in his pockets as he deliberated and trod one humpback to the next like crossing a creek on stones.

"Why are you saying strange things today?"

"I could be out to sea too long."

"But there is no sea."

"Now you're making my point for me."

Nobel pushed through a bed of crab grass, each blade swathed in verglas. If the seeds of a Eurasian weed could find their way here how could anything of animal force be kept away.

"I know that I like waking up with you and Mamma upstairs, and knowing that I'll see the critters we have. I don't know what else there is, but what I imagine from what I've read and you and Mamma have read to me, and what I know by listening to you."

"There's other ways to know."

"You're making me uncomfortable. You haven't talked this way to me before."

"Maybe that's the gift of getting older."

"You can keep it then."

Nobel laughed and the boy pulled a finger from a hawthorn branch.

"I think about the earth we're on sometimes and how it's so big it looks level when its round, and how little that means I am, here with you. You've said it's getting smaller to Mamma, and I don't know how that could be, but you're probably taking freedoms."

"There's truth to it."

"If I'm to be getting bigger and it's becoming smaller, then are we to meet?"

"That's the wresting unknown."

"Will that be belonging?"

"I don't know."

"Do you belong?"

"I'm answering that as we speak."

The boy gripped the twig like it was a divining wand that might lead him to words that could please them both.

"Ask me again, Papa."

Nobel stopped before their descent.

"Let whatever raises come out of you. Alright?"

The boy's eyes were like a dog's anticipating a ball to be tossed.

"Why should you live, boy?"

"Because I am," he barked from his belly, in a way that made Nobel step back.

The boy panted open-mouthed like a descendant of wolves, invoking a yowl to overtake him. Nobel wanted to cry out first that they might caterwaul together and be freed in their bawling, but the boy caught on a thought and the moment passed.

"Why are we taking my things to the waters?"

Nobel clutched the barrow handles, leaned back to control the slope and allowed the decline to do his work.

"The marsh is high so we'll get in easily."

"With the boat?"

"Yes."

"You know I don't like the boat."

"I do know. You can wait on shore."

"I don't like the shore either."

"Only because you walked out on the muskeg once. I'll show you where to step."

"And when to stop?"

"If I knew that we'd be speaking of lighter things."

Nobel was making a joke but felt hollow, like his chest was a steel drum. The boy looked confused.

The path twined its way past the occasional dogwood and witch hazel bare for the winter to a pond that fingered the tupelo gums and at high water touched the swampland miles away. Nobel recalled the dogwood blossoms, with their pinched petal tips withdrawing into the shape of a heart. It was a comfort for him as a boy, until his father taught him the tree's favored use in crucifixion and told him to look at the flower's shape and see sacrifice.

"Do you think someone might come? Is that why we're hiding my things?"

"No one can say what's on its way. We're just banking our ounce of prevention."

The rowboat was where Nobel'd left it, both oars tucked underneath. He'd worried the heavy rains of the last two winters had brought the waterline up enough to float it off.

"How deep is it, the waters?"

"Two men standing one atop another couldn't keep a nose above."

The boy helped Nobel right the boat, and they unpacked the barrow into it. The chain was too heavy even for two of them, so they moved it in portions. While firm on land, Nobel wrapped the sack with it like a roast in butcher's twine and tied the ends in a crude knot. Then he and the boy rolled the stuffed jute like a body over the transom and rested it on the gunwale.

"Will you come with me, boy?"

"No."

Together they pushed the loaded keel to the pond's lip and broke a translucent skin that dissolved like a mirage as the dinghy made a parting wake.

"Is it my company you're avoiding?"

"No. The water's too big."

"This water?"

"Yes." The boy nodded.

"This puddle? A city of men could micturate a bigger pool."

"I don't know what *micturate* is but I'm not going in."

"The planet is drowned with oceans and seas big enough to coat the moon ten times, with a thousand of these ponds stacked on one another. Waters so deep straight down the tallest mountain ever known to a man would need another half to touch a toe."

"This planet?"

"The very same."

"Stop making up stories to scare me."

"They're as real as we're standing here."

The boy looked like Columbus at the helm of the Santa Maria, staring at a waterfall flowing over the edge of the planet.

"I'm not in the mood to be fooled."

"I'm not doing so."

"Those are just in storybooks, the giant waters and mountaintops and their odd creatures."

"No. They're the grandeurs of this globe."

The boy's face wrinkled around his gape and Nobel awoke like a boy himself, on stage with a light burning on his nakedness, scrutinized by an audience that would never be pleased.

"Boy, I'm going to tell you the truth."

The boy dug his heels.

"I'm grasping for faith." Nobel stared at the sludge stretching up the boy's shoes, and pictured a man frozen before his crawl reached the fire. "There's just something between it and me."

"What something?"

"I wish I knew."

"Is it the beast?"

"It may be."

"Are you afraid of it?"

A hollow carapace fluttered in the wash, its pincers clamped on a stick as if to prove something. Stubbornness didn't require guts, for crawfish or men, Nobel thought.

"The ghost that inhabits me is who I'd be, if the unknown could be trusted. I fear, child, that rather than facing it, I've spread this affliction."

Nobel watched the boy shift from one foot to the other, struggling to understand, and wondered what he himself had always needed to hear, but never had.

The slosh drummed the hull like a knocking on Nobel's shell to come in.

"Boy. Who you are is a power no other person should hold."

"Are you saying goodbye or still trying to trick me into joining you?"

The boy was doing his best to look sturdy, but shook like a puppy broke free from a doomed litter. In the boy's mind, one mistake and a hand would descend and put him in the sack as well. Nobel knew that belief, intimately enough to forget it was always there.

"There's a photo of me your age, standing on a lake edge like that."

"Did you go in the boat?"

"I survived."

Needle ice sprouted from the clay in ribbons behind the boy, each stem capped in a floret of soil pretending to be alive. If only a great thumb and forefinger would deliver him by his scruff in the boy's place, Nobel thought. How else could he stop?

"Keep my coat for your shivering."

The boy took it and put it on. He looked like a nun in a habit.

"Why did you leave the others, Papa?"

"To elect a reason would belittle us both, a single event doesn't make a person."

Black frost had decayed the watercress and swamp rose into a tide of snails yanked from their pods that sprawled around them like his whorl uncoiled.

"The agreement is no one can change the world, yet it changes because of us."

There was nothing else to say.

He shoved off and left the boy a solitary missionary on the hummock.

TWENTY-SEVEN

Three years ago

Nobel could hear all five panting souls in his home, his own included.

The boy slept between them. He was small enough to tuck against either without being a nuisance. Olea preferred him in the cradle of her armpit. The child's warmth was like nothing else. Only a young animal came close, Nobel thought, and couldn't recall if he had a thermal power at the boy's age, and doubted it was noticed if he had. How many miracles decayed on the vine because a consciousness failed to pick them with attention? Was awareness the key to a realm apart from the drudge, he wondered, the kingdom of things like a child's heat?

Insomnia and old age were humiliating him, he concluded, to keep his mind off the question at hand.

He'd nailed the men's cargo boxes closed but animals would get in eventually, followed by carrion beetles, weevils and maggots, and finally bacteria and rainwater until it was an installation of rusting steel and the permanence of bone the weeds would carpet over, if he abandoned that portion of field. It would take years before it couldn't be spotted from the air. If someone came looking he wouldn't be able to talk his way out of it, even if he hid under a dunce cap.

It was better nothing was found, weapons and shells included. It would take a backhoe and crew of men a week to dig and refill a hole big enough. A man his age with a shovel could do it in three or four months, if he did nothing else. He could load the fuselage with their evidence and use the horses to pull it all and the wing pieces into the hickories. Fallen limbs would be the only camouflage, a cheesecloth coat at best.

If he could make it to the dry runnel, it was a rocky two hundred yards through the narrow stand, but the cleft would do most of the work for him. The canopy of inkberry would keep its secrets even in winter. He'd comb every paint chip from the field, plow and plant winter wheat.

It could be done because it had to be, he thought, and counted fusty inhalations from the shackled prisoners in the other room like sheep, with the maple savor of burnt Canadian bills in his sinuses.

TWENTY-EIGHT

Nobel could see the boy from the porch. The child was already at his chores, carting the previous day's waste to the compost and pigs.

"I respect your desire to protect us from whatever you found with those two, Mason." She didn't look up, but that wasn't the end of her thought. "So I'll let you conduct this at your own measure, but I can't see a good end."

She had right to question him, but he wasn't ready to let her know. The sound of chain shifting on wood jangled from the mudroom. It was like being heckled by a specter, he thought.

"Their trial's done. We're just waiting on the sentence."

"And all the words ever twisted won't summon your answer."

"Not once have I entered the ring with you and rated the favored fighter."

"Compliment me all you want, Judge. I still have to pull twice the eggs from our hens until you solve this puzzle, and we have men in our home."

The boy's shoes rapped on the porch steps and Nobel followed him inside.

He'd finished quicker than usual and his lip floated crooked over his top teeth.

"Have your routines changed?"

"No."

"So what's got you jaunty?"

"You're asking me what's not the same?"

He didn't expect an answer, Nobel realized.

"Buenos dias, Capitán?" The pilot sounded like a rested man and the boy slowed.

"Go in your room and have at your reading."

"Can I read to the visitors?"

"If they can hear you from your closed quarters, I can't stop it."

The boy shared the room beside theirs. It had been Nobel's library. Shelves of books lined two of the walls still, filled mostly with Olea's collection. The rest crowded boxes in the closet.

The pilot gave the boy a wink from the floor like a sunning gator, and the boy smiled and shut his door.

The copilot wasn't as jovial and moaned like a one-man infirmary.

"As pleasant as a bird's song, no?"

"One of you dropped this when you tumbled." Nobel set the pillbox on the floor within the pilot's reach. "I presume whatever's in there will shut his beak."

"Indeed, gracias."

The pilot opened the canister and revealed a store of green pills.

"I'll give you 900,000 loonies, give or take the fire damaged, to split those like Romeo and Juliet." Nobel said as he lowered himself into a Carver chair near the hearth.

"Why not force us? Like you would a horse."

"My horse is dead."

"As you keep reminding me."

The copilot accepted a pill on his tongue like a communion wafer. The way they were cuffed together the pilot had to squat. He pinched a tablet for himself and snacked on it like he was picking mites from an offspring's scalp.

"So tell me, what is it you are hiding, Capitán, that you have not telephoned your government?"

"I'm concealing the fact that I don't have a phone."

The pilot laughed, until his broken rib shut him up.

Nobel put his feet up on what remained of the banded hundreds.

"You have no need for money, even with the niño?"

"We tried feeding him currency. He didn't take to it."

The pilot chuckled again, to the limit of his pain threshold.

It was hard to discern who had the upper hand, Nobel thought.

"Americans are so interesting. Don't you think? At our meeting you would have shot us and felt at peace because we maintained our weapons. Now you cannot, yet we remain just as threatening."

"Our moral compass is prejudice in certain moments. It otherwise aims at potential."

"Yes. You are optimists."

"It could be said."

"A convenient-" the pilot paused. "What is the word for the drug a man of power feeds to weaker men to give them the illusion of choice?"

"Bromide."

"Si. That is it." The pilot contorted until he was comfortably prone. "A man from a pessimistic culture would have burned us in the plane, if he was confident no one would come looking for him."

"Lucky for you, I'm not Canadian."

The pilot grinned and the boy broke their standoff in a remedial staccato, "*Well, three or four months run along, and it was well into the winter, now. I had been to school most all the time, and could spell, and read, and write just a little.*" Clear enough for anything crouched within a mile to follow, Nobel thought, and Olea arrived with breakfast served in tins without cutlery.

For a week's time Nobel danced with the pilot as mongoose and serpent, waiting for guidance that never came.

Olea fed the men with the family, and the boy sat with the pilot as often as allowed.

Nobel dug a hole beside his decomposing mare and used the living one to pull her in, and spent his days clearing the men's every trace.

He didn't bury the human dead but left them their plywood caskets as planned to reprieve them the ape's desecration. After dark, he burned it all in the ravine and then dowsed the smoke before dawn with mud and wet blankets. He repeated the ritual five nights in a row. It was violent and untidy, but still a funeral rite for the couple, and the ash was left to carbonate the wild plants.

The copilot was on his feet by the seventh day and the pilot removed his bandage and found a scab going to scar. Nobel caught the men measuring their wounds in the window's reflection, and the pilot impulsively fondled the shrinking crater in his cheekbone that Nobel's bullet had chipped out.

They believed they'd been touched, he deduced, overhearing their murmurs.

They were devils that fell from the sky and alighted on grim prospects, miraculously restored and there was only one angel in sight.

Nobel saw reverence begin to inform the way they looked at the boy.

It was a gaze, not unlike love, he'd seen conmen award a patsy, as they visualized fortunes unloading into their pockets. Sevens aligned across their foreheads, Nobel imagined, as their eyes followed his six-year-old golden goose.

Olea didn't miss the shift. They gave the boy the unspoken respect one might an extraterrestrial.

Nobel was balancing them on a rope above the inferno.

TWENTY-NINE

Present Day

There was logic behind it of course. You can't hide a child from those who'd take him, if his evidence is undeniable.

Olea stood in the boy's empty room. She might have believed that was Nobel's motive if she hadn't been here before.

Eliminating the boy's effects was his way of preparing her.

Ironically it was the boy's affect that had them on the ledge, and that couldn't be removed. Nobel'd broken the furniture into tinder and the three of them had hauled the summer sofa down and set the room to look like cellar storage.

Her home was a carcass. She'd lived in the house without the boy for twenty years but it was intolerable now. When life left a thing, it couldn't be put back. We all learned that as small children, and who ever found reconciliation?

A single filament of silk connected her to what came next. She knew it was faith, but not that the past was as out of reach, and held by the same thread.

Olea bent down and ran her hand over the floor. Nobel'd

washed it to delete even the boy's spoor. She crawled on her knees and swept her fingers around the furniture and boxes and into every corner, searching for a hair from his head. There were none, and she sat on her knees and caught her breath. Being a lawman had inadvertently taught him how to clean, but he couldn't have erased the boy completely.

Where had he made a mistake?

She scrutinized each tread as she climbed.

They'd gone through every box, crawl, hiding place and square foot of the house and outbuildings together and Nobel had done a second pass alone.

The bathroom and kitchen could double as operating rooms, she thought, and the image made her rush to the bedroom.

The body of her sewing chair was as good as a secret compartment. Her basket was hidden in the chamber beneath the seat. There would be fabric, sections from the boy's old clothes that she'd saved as patches.

As she unclasped the cushion, her weight sunk. She knew by the compartment's order, her store was gone. Nobel stayed her equal, and had the advantage of practice. There wasn't a fiber left to represent the boy.

Olea fingered her bobbins, imagining there might be a string of the child to touch. It was as if he'd never existed. She pulled a needle from its sheath in a spool and returned it to its proper slot and closed the chair. Why had she left it in red, of all colors?

She didn't realize she was running until she'd almost reached the horse manger.

The swallow hatchling that fell from the barn gutter that summer, it had landed on the hayshed. The boy'd heard its cheeping and scaled the trough, wearing her old evening gloves to save the chick from his scent. He'd waved victorious from the roof. On his way down he'd caught his shirt and a patch was lost. She knew, because it took one to mend it.

Nobel hadn't done any work near there, had he? Not since the snow broke through the thatch last winter. It was bright red. It would attract nesters, but that season wasn't for months. The piece should still be there.

Olea put a foot up on the fence rail and gripped the barn wall as she scavenged the melting slime. She knew where it had to be. She'd watched the boy clamber down, but there was no trace of him. Barn mice were notorious for stealing anything soft to build their beds.

Please don't let another thing beat me, Olea said aloud and probed her bare hands through the frosted jelly of algae that glazed the wood.

It wasn't there.

The boy is gone, she muttered and slipped, and her thumb freed a brick of frozen mulch. It fell instead of her, she thought, as it spattered into a gel of dead oak leaves and lichen.

Behind it was the sprig of cloth, pinched in the wood like a rose petal.

Olea entered the house and felt the cold when her fingers fumbled the clips on the back of the picture frame. They'd numbed so thick, she didn't notice she'd popped her skin until she saw the blood.

The photograph of Nobel and Cole hadn't been moved in so long there was a stain of color where it had protected the wallpaper.

She wasn't the first to hide a treasure in plain sight. It was also the one thing in the house she knew Nobel would never touch.

With the longer of her nails she was able to pry the small

flat of wood from the frame's back and reveal its innards. There was a photo of a baby boy there with *Cole, two years old* written on the backside, three folded newspaper clippings, and a hair ribbon that was the only thing her mother had left behind besides her two daughters.

She'd intended to look at nothing, simply put the piece of the boy with the others and reseal the tomb, but her baby was smiling at her and her hands were opening the articles before she could stop them.

County Judge Resigns In Deal To Protect Son was one of the headlines, above a diptych of Nobel in his gown and Cole handcuffed, screaming at a deputy. It was the last time they'd be seen together. The second declaimed *Cole Nobel Kills Again* above the image of a sedan pitched forward and horseshoed on a tree. She didn't need to read either. She knew them by heart.

It was the third newsprint image she was after, like a dog going for a porcupine its face already covered in quills. *Third Grade Class Picture Indicts County Prosecutor*, the headline read over a grade school photo, faded but each smile as bright as when it was taken. Even the one worn by the boy in the front row that the paper had circled, holding the hand of the boy next to him.

Her moralizing was a charade. They'd already killed a child.

Olea squeezed the red scrap of cloth between her finger and thumb, and recognized the boy in the photographs of her son. Why are we secretly guided by our violations, rather than our moments of bliss? It was a flaw in nature that favored the wound. She didn't close the frame. Instead she removed its picture and added it to the others.

If Nobel had cleaned so thoroughly, he didn't intend the boy to return.

THIRTY

Three years ago

Before the household woke, the pilot used a stone hidden beneath the molding to grind his remaining opiates into powder, and then slept through Nobel's morning chores.

The two men were returned enough, Nobel had drawn a charcoal line on the floor and staked an arc out back, to mark their chain's reach.

They'd taken two tigers as pets, and each waited patiently to catch a back turned.

Nobel could see them both from where he stood in the kitchen. The copilot had made a game of kicking a dried pea like a ball with his fingers, and was doing so now.

"This needs to be finished." Olea had one eye on the boy outside and one on Nobel.

"I am aware."

"There'll be no talk of going to the authorities."

"Did we become Pinkertons without my knowing it?"

"Don't start saddling your high-horse. From what you've

inferred, they'd both get the chair."

"So I should shoot them like butcher hogs?" Nobel rinsed his hands in the sink. "In the forehead or the back?"

"You can hang them with pink tea cozies on their heads, if it makes you feel better."

"Now you're just being brassy. Let's not bet it all on a feeling. You're not a cornered mother."

"Aren't I?"

Nobel watched the boy chasing a chicken outside.

"A hanging's not pretty. The body moves about, shaking. The dying often lose themselves from every opening during their choke. Their last cackle will make you sleep differently."

He'd shared custody on Kansas executions and she knew he'd seen the last hanging in Missouri at too young an age thanks to his father.

"I'll dig the holes then, Judge. You just kneel them before each."

"In front of the pig trough will make the murders tougher to prove." He could tell she was growing tired of their banter. "You're imagining it like you've seen it dramatized. It won't be that way."

Olea shook the pan she was working as if to keep her mind from slowing.

"It's not like you haven't done it before."

"When forced by instinct."

"Let it do so again."

"I would but I prefer my knuckles not to drag when I walk."

"Should I offer the swarthier one my throat? Would that do?"

Nobel rinsed the dishes she'd finished with to occupy his hands.

"Clearly you are in my life to show me I can survive defeat."

"You'd have them live, after what you know?"

Regardless of his reasoning, the truth was he simply didn't want to kill anyone.

"There's a gap between wanting them dead, and wanting to do the killing. You know what that gap is called?"

"What?"

"Civilization."

It was tens steps to the shotgun. Olea could take the skull from both men in under a minute, if she stood by her argument. It not being woman's work didn't hold water.

The way Nobel was looking at her, he'd heard her thoughts. She didn't look up as she plated their hominy and eggs.

"So you see yourself roping the two of them to one horse and riding the other into town like a bounty hunter out of the old west?"

"Not as you're saying it, but in so many words."

"The whole world won't want to get involved, when they learn about the two of them?" He didn't answer. "You ride them in, a man your age, it'll be the biggest story going. You'll be a celebrity in Japan. The local and national agencies will want to see what they brought with them too. You'll have yourself a regular barnburner in front of every camera they can squeeze onto our porch, explaining why you barbecued it all."

"I can say they did it, covering their tracks. We took them by surprise, before they'd got away."

"Have you returned to infancy? Would you believe that?"

Nobel saw the debate getting away from him and studied the countertop as his rejoinder.

"You really think we'll be able to keep the boy from all the people who will come? And them from him?"

"We'll hide him somehow."

"With investigators scouring our property for weeks? He'll be the first thing those two mention."

"Maybe."

"Surely."

"I haven't given up on it all and that's the end of it."

He knew his tone implied that she had and watched her pan scraping slow.

"I'm not protecting my ideals, Nobel, I'm defending our lives. What are you doing?"

"Defending a place worth living in."

Olea put their plates in the oven to punctuate the stalemate.

"For all you know they have connections. Some government official who doesn't consider your eyes worth looking at will grant them immunity and we'll get a visit soon after."

"Even if they don't and end up in prison or the chair, there's a good chance others will be coming for us."

"How will we protect the boy then?"

"I do not know."

The copilot laughed loudly at himself and Nobel caught the pilot staring at him. They were out of earshot, but it was possible he could lipread.

"They'll be devising their own escape soon, Mason. If they haven't already."

"I'm aware."

"They'll grab me or the boy as soon as we drop our wits."

He knew this was true as well.

"If they threatened our lives?"

"They don't yet."

"Yet?"

"I'm not a man who can see the future, Olea!"

He'd raised his voice and regretted it.

"I may remind you that you said that one day."

Olea took a plate for the boy and left Nobel staring at nothing.

They'd given each a small bag of cornhusk to rest on and left them their evening meal overnight, and there was no dog. Those were their mistakes, he realized too late.

THIRTY-ONE

The men's evening rations sat at the brink of the charcoal ring.

The pilot had solved the puzzle days ago, when he discovered part of a floorboard had gone soft. He only needed the time to put each piece in its place.

Each night he fidgeted before bed, until their sleeping position put the copilot's legs over the rotting fir and the chain where it wouldn't be disturbed. He feigned colic as well and abandoned the end of his meal.

The co-pilot distrusted the leavings at first and ate only a bite the second night, but by the third he'd become accustomed to their routine and licked the tin shiny.

They were never far apart, the pilot's right hand cuffed to the copilot's right ankle, even during bowel breaks, which they'd learned to share outside like a menses.

They had no choice but to sit close to one another for meals.

The copilot took his portion and when his eyes were in his

dish, the pilot mixed the powder into his own dinner and went about eating around it.

By the time he was through the copilot was shuffling like a sow, and grabbed the pilot's plate the moment he paused.

"Gracias."

"No hay de que."

The pilot knew there wasn't enough narcotic left to kill a man, but it would sedate the copilot's squeals, and once the house was dark and silent he counted the beats between the other's breaths until they conjoined in a deep rhythm.

Without making a sound, he shoved a sock into the copilot's gullet and covered his face with a pillow, and then knelt with his feet clamped on it. Clutching the copilot's arms and legs, he fought the bucking body until it shuddered like a drowned piglet and stopped.

As the sleepers whistled, he chipped through the rotten floor wood and stuck the copilot's foot into the hole. The calf muffled in a pillow, he braced the ankle against the joist like a stick held over a table's ledge, dropped his weight, and snapped the shinbones.

Their dishes were old aluminum, the sort a prospector used. Crouched in the dark, the pilot folded his, bending it until the friction softened the metal. Then he ripped it in half, and with the edge filleted the skin around the copilot's shin and pulled back the flesh and fat. Blood spurted his face and warmed his fingers as he cut through the tendons and vessels and sawed through the steaming muscle until the foot slid off the cuff and dropped under the house.

Nobel stored his rifle on two boat spikes above the closet near his bed and he opened his eyes in time to see the shadow of its stock crack his forehead.

Through a blur of blood, he watched the pilot kneel on

Olea's chest and strike her face until her cheekbones collapsed and jaw split. Then he drug her to the floor by a heel. The hint of sun sheened his mask as he made a noose of Nobel's belt and hoisted her up on one of the spikes like a gallows.

Nobel fought dizziness to free himself from his blankets as the pilot shut the belt in the closet jam. Olea swung like a pendulum bob, her face bloated and red as she clawed at her throat.

"Say something funny now, Capitán."

The shotgun was on a rack behind the stove. If he could just get to it. Nobel got his legs off the bed, and the pilot cut through his scalp and ear with the shorn tin dish.

"That is for my dead friend."

Nobel fell to his knees and pressed his lobe to stop the gush.

"He was a psychopath, but loyalty is not judgmental."

Olea kicked and pulled at the leather that crushed her windpipe. She would die the moment she tired.

"Cut her down and I'll start the car for you."

"That is very generous. It is a deal."

Nobel could make out the remaining straps of Canadian in a sackcloth at the pilot's feet and the boy gagged and calf-tied behind him.

"I will cut her down for you, as soon as she is dead." The pilot leveled the rifle and pulled the trigger.

The explosion was like a cannon in the room. The bullet cut through Nobel's thigh and clanged in the hollow.

"Can you still hear me, Capitán?"

Nobel's vision spun like he was a pinwheel as Olea flopped, slapping the doorframe, and the pilot collected the shotgun and shoved it and Nobel's rifle toe-first into the stove.

"What did you do with my gun? The gold one."

"Buried it."

"That is unfortunate."

Both gunstocks charred and smoked as their chrome-moly rosed.

"You failed as a lawman, no?" A smile filled the pilot's gory bobblehead. "Si. I have always been good at reading people."

Nobel skated on the slick beneath him, unable to grip the floor.

"You were wrong, Capitán. There is no boss waiting for me, because I am the boss. I just have a poor man's teeth."

Olea retched and caught the closet doorknob with a foot.

"I castrated the man you found in the box in front of my wife. Then I had my associate give her his head and the head of her pet to hold, and I cut off her head myself. She believed she could make me a- What is the word?"

"A cuckold."

"That is it. You are a good talker, Capitán. I bet you are an even better thinker. There is a famous statue of you, do you know it? It is of a person who does nothing but sit."

Olea got her second foot on the handle and by twisting opened the door. The belt released, she dropped and her arm splintered as she hit the wood.

Nobel stretched toward her like a swimmer in a pool.

The pilot watched them in reverie, two crushed insects reaching through their guts as their baby wriggled in a bird's mouth.

"I will tell you what your father failed to. It is the reason you are here." The pilot shouldered the wrap of cash and eclipsed the sunrise. "The child who runs from his shadow is never safe," he said and picked up the boy by his roped limbs. "The child who becomes his shadow is a man."

"Send me a postcard if you ever get there."

The pilot grinned at Nobel like a brat who didn't care for his present.

"Without this child, I suspect you will not survive to receive it."

The boy squalled through his gag and the pilot walked out, carrying him like a suitcase.

THIRTY-TWO

The boy's wailing echoed outside like funeral pipes as Nobel's hands slipped on the black puddle growing beneath him, a spider trapped in a bowl.

"Lie on your back."

The room flared with light and whirled like a carnival ride but he did as she asked.

"Pull yourself under the bed."

Each word was a chunk of glass wedged in her throat. Olea's nose was stuffed with blood and her jawbone and voice box were crushed like a can.

Nobel found the bed slats and tugged himself beneath, climbing a ladder nailed to a turning wheel.

The pilot was chopping at the locked garage with Nobel's pickaxe. The posts had brown rot and the hinges would give soon.

"Can you see?"

"As good as a mole."

"Reach up." Olea caught her reflection in the floor mirror. Her face was a red morel, plums of blood had formed around her eyes, and a shard of bone made a tent on her arm.

It was silent outside. The pilot had quieted the boy and he'd gotten in.

Olea crawled toward the window like an inchworm.

"Did you find it?"

"I did."

Nobel felt a strip of canvas sewn into the mattress and the rumble of both garage doors towed over the grit. The battery would be drained but if the pilot got it rolling it could start.

Olea tucked a foot under her good hip.

Nobel yanked off the patch. If the car wouldn't run, he'd steal the horses. The mattress had a cut in it and he pushed his hand inside. The weight and cold of the metal could only be a handgun. He didn't question her, just slid it across the floor.

Olea caught the revolver and heaved her body onto the chest of drawers. The pistol was in poor condition when she'd found it underground tangled in their potatoes and looked decrepit now. She jammed its barrel through the window glass.

The pilot had the car out of the garage. He was closing the trunk on the boy as the shatter drew his attention.

She was quite the sight, a mangled old woman propped on one working arm, clutching a firearm goofy gripped as she used the window rail to align the front and rear sites. The pilot was more confused than afraid and Olea pulled the trigger.

"It would be better to throw it or beat your husband with it perhaps, señora."

"Nobel?"

"The hammer caught up or the firing pin was faulty."

"You Americans," the pilot chuckled and put a hand on the open trunk lid. "Of all the drugs in the world, your favorite is hope."

With a wink, he tipped an imaginary hat and Olea pulled again.

The bullet burst his nose and left a crater as it punched through his brain and erupted out the back of his skull in a buttercup of pelt, bone and black hair.

THIRTY-THREE

Present day
___

The air was like inhaling a chest of bees.

She'd run the distance from the house and could barely breathe.

It wasn't far to where their trail disappeared over the peak, and she envisioned Nobel holding the boy's corpse. She could see the boy's skin dulling as gravity lured his blood toward the soil, his schoolboy face a piecrust tossed on a skeleton with holes cut for the eyes, both cloudy oysters, plastic in a stillness that meant he was gone.

She reached the decline's edge and was hit with a cataract of white that matched the sky.

The boy stood at the shore in a coat that fit him like a cassock.

Nobel was twenty yards adrift in the rowboat.

The boy heard her steps before she spoke.

"Go home now."

The slope gave Olea a forced waddle, like he'd read penguins had. She trod through the melting glop and stopped before him.

"Finish your chores. If we don't return before dark, sleep in our bed, but feed the stove first."

"I don't understand."

"If we don't return tomorrow, do what needs to be done for yourself."

"Why are you being weird?"

"You've seen me prepare your food and Nobel's taught you to care for the animals. If you get low on stock, it's okay to kill a chicken."

"I don't want to."

"I don't think you'll have to. There's more than enough in the pantry to last you the winter."

"You're scaring me."

"Boy."

Nobel was paddling back to shore.

"You know how to keep the fire going."

The boy understood it wasn't a question. Olea watched her breath turn to steam and disappear before it reached him.

"Child?" Her voice started a crack that passed through her as Nobel stuck an oar into the sludge to ease his landing.

"Enjoy your adventure."

The rowboat skid ashore and Nobel stood. The bog swilled and heaved an umber froth. Nothing was said between them and he didn't know how, but this was goodbye.

"Last chance to brave this piddler's tarn," he said and stepped into the mere to help Olea aboard.

The boy said nothing and she straddled the breasthook and sat on the stern thwart.

Nobel stretched out for the boy to give him purchase and the boy walked into the water and took his hand. Rimed waves of silt flowed over their shoes at the pulse of a ballast emptying of sand.

"Boy. What you can do, the magic in you."

Nobel held one hand to the boat and the other to the boy.

"People are going to want it, but that's not who you are."

The boy rooted his feet and the surge swashed his ankles.

"You're a good boy. The bad is in the world. Do your best not to let it in."

Tears spilled down the boy's cheeks and joined the slush. The ground began to pop its glass husk like a hatchling stretching its shell, and Nobel gripped his fingers, and climbed into the boat.

THIRTY-FOUR

A sheep's wool of mist curled on the pond's surface. The shore would soon disappear.

Sarvisberry shoots stretched from the alluvium verge to the crest, crowding the path. Each branch proffered a secret galaxy of buds that would lantern winter's end in swarms of fireflies. The boy stood atop this potential. Nobel postponed his rowing and Olea turned to see.

He imagined the sight from the peak, as the boy watched them vanish. Two ghosts evaporating into the fog, then they were gone.

She faced him from the stern as he carved their wake.

Except for the dip of the oars and whine of the rowlocks, they could be paddling the seas of the moon.

"He once asked me why we aren't out stopping the slavery that exists."

"What did you tell him?"

"A man takes care of his family and his fellow man. The

order is his dilemma."

He wrenched the oars as if he were opening a set of doors to exit.

"You were going to drown him."

Every stubborn belief hid a truth the holder couldn't look at and survive, he thought, instead of speaking.

"To protect him from his fellow man, or his fellow man from him?"

Nobel slowed his sculling and his paddles mimicked the flap of wings.

"I've done neither."

He found her eyes.

"But you knew he was afraid of the water, and wouldn't go with you."

To be freed of his conscience, that was the gift he'd never receive. Cypress knees gathered at the shoal in a herd of swamp creatures, poking up their heads to scrutinize him.

"You're still a man."

Of all the words those were the last he wanted to hear. They'd reached their depth and he took the oars into the boat.

"Why did you never ask about the pistol I hid years ago?"

"You did it to fortify us, against my sense of duty."

A stem of muskgrass coiled the oar throat on her side in a necklace of darter eggs, and she shook her head.

"I shed my skin when I met you. I feared the moment you didn't cover me."

The bow breached as he sat beside her, the chained sack perched between them.

"I sent a letter to the county office."

If Nobel was surprised he didn't show it.

"Someone will care for him?"

"And the animals."

"If they ignore it?"

"He'll walk to the road."

Olea took the stack of newsprint, fabric and the small portrait photo from her coat pocket and set them on top of the boy's things. Nobel put his hand down on the photographs.

The picture of Cole as an infant stared at him from the top of the pile.

He'd learned it before but it didn't take, so life had cornered him. You can't escape what you fear, because it is you.

Olea placed her hand onto his.

She was wearing his manacles as a bracelet. The other half dangled like a tire swing.

Tails of drifting milfoil wagged on the swell, and she tucked his end of the cuffs beneath the links and closed it on his wrist.

Fanworts bundled in sprays at the sternpost, and uprooted dollar bonnets assembled in witness along the strake, each exposed belly glinting with mucilage.

The sack was balanced on the seat plank, against the boat's sheer at its fulcrum, and was top-heavy. A nudge and it would be overboard like an anchor to the bottom.

He gripped her fingers and her voice clung to him.

"Will it be cold?"

"I will keep you warm."

Swirls of vapor mantled the boat until they were inside a cloud. Olea touched their baby and the bag fell, and took them underwater.

On his knees in the black chill, Nobel pulled her into his arms and felt hers wrap his neck. Her forehead pressed against his and she held tight as he breathed her like water into his lungs. So were the lucky born, she thought at last.

CITATIONS:

Marcel Proust, *In Search of Lost Time*, Vol. VI: The Sweet Cheat Gone, Ch. I: "Grief and Oblivion", (1925): *"On ne guérit d'une souffrance qu'à condition de l'éprouver pleinement."* *("We are healed of a suffering only by experiencing it to the full")*

Mark Twain, *Adventures of Huckleberry Finn*, Chapter 4, (1885): *"Well, three or four months run along, and it was well into the winter, now. I had been to school most all the time, and could spell, and read, and write just a little."*

Alfred, Lord Tennyson, *Maud and Other Poems*, Maude, (1855): *"There has fallen a splendid tear, from the passion-flower at the gate. She is coming, my dove, my dear; She is coming, my life, my fate; The red rose cries, 'She is near, she is near;' And the white rose weeps, 'She is late;' The larkspur listens, 'I hear, I hear;' And the lily whispers 'I wait.'"*

The Holy Bible, King James Version, New York: Oxford Edition, (1769): John 15:19 *"If ye were of the world, the world would love his own: but because ye are not of the world, but I have chosen you out of the world, therefore the world hateth you."* Matthew 4:24 *"and they brought unto him all sick people that were taken with divers diseases and torments, and those which were possessed with devils, and those which were lunatick..."* Deuteronomy 12:20-21 *"This our son is stubborn and rebellious, he will not obey our voice; he is a glutton, and a drunkard.' And all the men of his city shall stone him with stones, that he die..."*

The Holy Bible, English Standard Version® (ESV®), (copyright © 2001, by Crossway, a publishing ministry of Good News Publishers. Used by permission.): Isaiah 14:21 *"Prepare slaughter for his sons because of the guilt of their fathers, lest they rise and possess the earth."*

Jude Baas has authored original, adapted and re-imagined feature films and developed original and source-based dramatic television series for seven major motion picture studios and networks. He now writes novels, short stories, plays and graphic novels in Portland, Oregon.

Visit him at JudeBaas.com
~ and ~
Facebook.com/authorJudeBaas

Made in the USA
Columbia, SC
06 December 2020